KIDNAPPED

Everyday Heroes Series Book Four

Margaret Daley

Kidnapped

Copyright © 2019 by Margaret Daley

All rights reserved. No part of this book may be reproduced in any form or by any electronic or mechanical means, including information storage and retrieval systems, without permission in writing from the author, except by a reviewer, who may quote brief passages in a review.

All texts contained within this document are a work of fiction. Any resemblance to actual events, locales or persons (living or dead), is entirely coincidental.

ONE

Beth Sherman sat in the front seat on a church bus, tired after a fun, activity-filled weekend at a lake retreat spent with twenty-five children from seven to twelve years old. Dusk was settling over the ranch lands along the two-lane highway. It would be dark by the time they returned to the parking lot at The Redeemer Church. All she wanted to do after spending forty-eight hours away from home was to go to sleep.

When she volunteered to be a chaperon, her first time since she'd come to Cimarron City, she should have asked her boss for Monday off so she could bounce back from an exhausting retreat.

She should have more energy. She needed an exercise routine, although she hated doing it. But if she was going to do this in the future—and she wanted to—then she needed to build up her stamina.

She glanced back at the children behind her. Nearly half of them were sleeping. Some of the others fought to keep their eyes from closing, but it didn't look like they would win the battle. She'd go to sleep, too, if she wasn't one of the five chaperons. Instead, she straightened in her seat and tried to keep her eyes on the road before the bus.

An oncoming van crested the hill moving toward them. The vehicle moved over the line and onto the shoulder of the road. The driver corrected, and Beth breathed a sigh. The relief was short-lived, as the van crossed the double yellow line in the road.

"Whoa," Sam, the bus driver, said and slowed.

Beth glanced out the side to her right. The shoulder there was brief with a slope that could cause the van to tip over.

Still, the driver eased off the road to give the van room to correct.

Beth tensed and glanced to see that the children in the back were okay. Her gaze was drawn beyond them through the back window.

An eighteen-wheeler barreled down on them.

A horn and a screech of brakes announced that the driver of the semi was alerted to what was happening.

Too late.

The semi swiveled and plowed into the rear of the bus—where all the duffle bags had been stored. The collision knocked Beth forward, her seatbelt keeping her in place.

Cries filled the air.

She'd turned to see how the children were, but only a couple of seconds later, the van rammed into the area where the truck and bus were touching. She was tossed in another direction. Her head struck against the window. Pain streaked down her.

Screams assaulted her. Dazed, Beth

fumbled to unsnap her seatbelt then pushed to her feet. As she pivoted toward the children behind her, her sudden movement caused her eyesight to flutter while dizziness attacked all her senses. She gripped the back of her seat while she assessed the damage to the others. Although her legs were shaky, she began making her way toward the rear where the impact was the worst, gripping whatever she could to keep herself upright.

As she checked the kids right behind her, an explosion rocked the bus. Her grasp tightened as her fingernails dug into the leather to keep her on her feet. Her gaze fixed on the flames shooting up from the van.

"We need to get off this bus now," Beth shouted over the wails and moans.

Spread throughout the bus, the other four chaperons were on their feet, except for Susie, who sat in the back. While the three adults helped the children exit with the bus driver's assistance, Beth checked and comforted whomever she could as she made her way to the rear where Susie lay against the back window, her eyes closed.

The fire spread toward the bus. Beth felt Susie's pulse and breathed a sigh of relief. Beth's surroundings were illuminated with the flames creeping nearer. She saw the blood running down the window. She had to carry Susie out of the bus. Now.

Beth struggled to move Susie to the end of the seat then stooped to cradle the woman against her chest. When Beth rose, she staggered back a few paces before something deep inside of her drew the strength she needed to the surface. She moved forward, glancing at the seats to make sure they were empty. When she reached the steps off the bus, the driver came into sight.

"Clara's missing," Sam halted at the bottom of the exit. "Did you see her?"

"No, but take Susie, and I'll go look for Clara."

"Sure." He climbed the steps and took hold of the injured woman. "Take my flashlight."

As soon as she could, Beth whirled around and headed back down the aisle, trying to remember where Clara had sat during the ride. Why hadn't she seen her earlier?

As she made her way toward the rear of the bus, she again searched every seat, even underneath each one with the flashlight. No one. Over the sound of the fire, Beth called out, "Clara, where are you?" What if she was hurt? But where? She'd look...

She remembered seven-year-old Clara had a favorite blanket that she'd brought on the trip and carried it around with her that first night. She'd never spent the night away from home and had been scared on Friday. Beth headed for the bags at the back. If she recalled, Clara had been sitting a couple of rows from where the suitcases were.

"Clara, I'm here to help you." Beth coughed as the smoke seeped into the interior of the bus. *Please, Lord, help me find her*.

"Beth, have you seen Clara?" Sam headed down the aisle.

Beth reached the stack of belongings.

KIDNAPPED

"Not yet."

"The fire's spreading."

She heard a noise coming from nearby. Crying? "Clara."

The weeping grew. Beth homed in on the sound and found Clara buried among the duffel bags, clutching her blanket. "Come on, sweetie. I'll take you out of here." Beth handed the flashlight to Sam then scooped up Clara and headed as fast as she could toward the exit.

When they were out of the bus and hurrying toward the group of children and chaperons, the resonance of a siren signaled help was on the way. Beth released a long sigh. With Clara clinging to her, Beth finally reached the others.

"We need to move further away." Sam pointed in the direction they should move.

Still holding Clara, Beth followed the group. Halfway there, another explosion blasted through the air, shaking the ground and taking Beth to her knees with Clara still in her arms.

* * *

The next day, Beth hobbled to the front entrance of her house and looked through her peephole to check who was outside. She smiled and opened the door. "Ann, it's good to see you."

Her neighbor, from two houses away, held up a casserole. "I've fixed you dinner."

Beth stepped to the side. "Come in."

"Where do you want me to put the dish?"

"In the refrigerator for later. I really appreciate the thought."

"How do you feel?" Ann opened the fridge, set the meal on the top rack, then shut the door.

"Okay."

Ann shook her head. "I don't believe you. You're limping. You have a knot on your forehead. I'd say you aren't all right."

"A few bumps and bruises. A doctor at the hospital checked me out. I'll be able to go to work tomorrow. Would you like coffee? I made a pot when I got up a few hours ago."

"If you let me get it for you."

Beth nodded and took a seat at her

kitchen table.

Ann poured the coffee into two mugs, brought Beth hers, then sat across from her. "I tried calling you before I came over, but it went to voicemail. I left a message so ignore it. I wanted to make sure you were all right."

"Thanks."

Beth's cell phone buzzed on the counter by the door into the hallway.

"You can get it. Don't mind me." Ann took a sip of her drink. "I'll enjoy this coffee. You make the best."

"That's okay. I started receiving calls at six this morning."

"Why?"

"Because I found a little girl and got her off the bus before it caught fire."

"I can understand people in town wanting to thank you, but six is a little early. Did you get any sleep last night?"

"A couple of hours. Most of the calls were from the media or people I don't know. At first, the ones I recognized from my friends, I answered them. But then it got to be too much. Too many were unknown callers."

"I found out you were hurt when I saw a photo of you on the early morning news. Not long after that I got a call from the pastor since he knew I lived nearby. He's at the hospital visiting with Susie and will come see you later."

"That's good to know. I'll be on the lookout for him. I can ignore the calls, but a couple of strangers have come to my door. I didn't let them know I was here. I don't like this attention."

"Get some sleep. I'll stay and make sure no one bothers you."

Beth shook her head. "You don't need—"

"Beth Sherman, let me do this for you. You look like you're going to fall asleep in that chair you're sitting in."

"I'm not the only one who got the kids off the bus. It was a group effort."

"But you stayed to find Clara. Fifteen minutes of fame is fleeting. It'll be over when the next news story comes along.

TWO

Four weeks later

Beth Sherman decreased her gait to a fast walk as she approached her home. Sweat beaded her forehead and stung her eyes. She came to a stop a few feet from her porch, drawing in deep breaths to slow her quick heartbeat. She hated exercising, but her job as an administrative assistant had her sitting a lot. Keeping active was important to her health, so she was trying various forms of exercise to find the one she could live with. Jogging wasn't going to be that for her. She would strike it off her list when she got inside.

As she swiped her hand across her forehead, she mounted the porch steps and stuck her hand into her small pocket to retrieve her key. She approached her door, coming to a halt a few feet away. Her heart jolted. The entrance was open a couple of inches. Her heartbeat revved up. She backed away and nearly stumbled down the stairs. She caught herself before she did.

I know I locked it before I went jogging. Someone's in my house.

She whirled around and ran toward the next-door neighbor's place on the left to call 9-1-1. She didn't bring her cell phone with her because she didn't want to deal with any calls. But now it would have been to her benefit if she had.

When she reached the front door, she rang the bell, her heart pounding inside her chest. No one answered. Mr. and Mrs. Jackson must still be at work. With a glance toward her home, Beth started for the next house on her left. Ann Maxwell was retired. Maybe she would be there.

Beth kept looking over her shoulder toward her yard. A man wearing black sweats and a hoodie hurried from her house. Her first impulse was to go after him, but he was too big for her to subdue. Instead, she ducked behind a thick bush near the Jacksons' porch before the intruder saw her.

A white SUV whipped around the corner and sped down the street. The driver slammed on the brakes in front of her house while the man in black raced to SUV.

The driver stomped on the accelerator, and the vehicle flew past Beth. She tried to see the license plate number, but a parked truck blocked her view. The SUV turned onto a side street and disappeared.

She crawled out from behind the bush and stood. Her body shook. She folded her arms across her chest to still the tremors. Glancing toward her house, she tried to decide what to do—go to her place and call the police or try to find someone at home to use their phone. What if an intruder was still around?

Shivering at the thought of someone being inside her home, she headed toward the house to the left of her neighbor. Ann went to her church and often volunteered there. She'd brought Beth a casserole after the bus accident. The truck that blocked her view of the license plate number was parked in front of her home, so Ann might be there.

As Beth headed to the porch, she paused and scanned her surroundings in case the guy and his driver returned. Although one of her neighbors at the end of the street was backing out of his driveway in his car, the rest of the area was quiet. She pressed the bell and prepared herself to run out into the road to flag down the man if Ann wasn't home.

She had turned to chase down the car when the front door opened. As she glanced over her shoulder, she came to a stop and swung around.

A tall man, over six feet with short dark brown hair and gray eyes dressed in a police uniform stood in the entrance. What if the person in her house had broken into this one first?

"Is Mrs. Maxwell all right?"

The police officer smiled. "Yes, she's

fine." He studied her face for a few seconds. "Are you all right?"

"Colby, who's at the door?" Behind him, Ann asked the man blocking the entrance.

"Ann, it's Beth." She leaned to the right to see around him.

"Is something wrong?" The older woman moved closer while the police officer stepped back to give her a full view of Beth.

"I need to use your phone to call the police," Beth looked into the man's gray eyes, "unless you can come and help me."

Ann touched Beth's arm. "Of course, Colby will help you. I can come too."

She shook her head. "Someone broke into my house." She looked at the older woman. "Ann, I don't want anything to happen to you."

Colby turned around. "Duke, come. She's right, Nana. You need to stay here."

He's Ann's grandson.

Ann stepped to the side while a black Rottweiler with splatters of brown trotted toward Colby. He grabbed a leash on a table in the entry hall and clipped the lead on the dog's collar. "I just finished my shift, but I can help you. What happened?"

Beth quickly recounted what occurred when she returned from her run. "The guy hopped into a white SUV. I couldn't tell you the license number or the make of the vehicle. It happened so fast."

"Which house is yours?" Ann's grandson asked as he moved past her onto the porch.

Beth faced him and pointed to her right. "The second house down. I'll show you."

"You and Nana should stay here until I make sure everything's okay." He turned to leave.

"I'll wait outside my house."

"No. Stay here," Colby said in an authoritative voice as he swung back around, his stiff body blocking her. "I need to keep my focus on making sure your place is safe for you to return to." His tone softened, his stance relaxed. "I'll call this in to the station. As soon as I clear your house, I'll let Nana and you know. Then you can come home."

Realizing the logic behind his words,

Beth nodded and gave him her key. "That's in case the man locked the door as he left."

As Colby strode away, Ann stepped to Beth's side. "He knows his job. Keeping people safe has been his mission in life since he was a young boy. I'm so glad he's returned to Cimarron City and is working with the police department."

"When did he come back?"

"Last Friday. He's staying with me until he finds a place to live. I'm trying to convince him to take his time. I have plenty of room here." As Ann entered her home, she waved her arm at the large living room and dining room. "I've missed him the past twelve years he worked in Tampa. He went to college there and stayed when he graduated with a degree in criminal justice."

"What brought him back to Oklahoma?" Beth took a seat in the chair across from Ann who eased onto the couch near an end table where her landline phone sat.

She frowned. "He'll deny this, but I think he returned because his heart's broken."

"He's divorced?"

Ann shook her head. "He had a girlfriend. They dated over a year. When I talked with Colby the last couple of months, I could tell something was wrong, but he never told me why they went their separate ways. But that isn't why I think his heart's still broken. He left Cimarron City because his fiancée was killed in a bank robbery. They both had graduated from the same high school and had dated for several years. He had been late meeting her at the bank, and he hasn't been able to move on."

Beth thought about her last serious relationship that ended six months ago. They had lived in the same apartment complex. Thomas hadn't been happy when she told him she didn't want to date him anymore. Not long after breaking it off with him, her tires had been slit, and her vehicle had been defaced with deep, long scratches. She'd moved across town to get away from him. Now she parked her car in the garage when she came home. Thomas hadn't bothered her since she'd moved, but what if Thomas was the guy who'd been in her house? Was this connected to the hang-up calls she'd received yesterday evening and again today at work? Since the bus crash, she'd gotten a lot of calls. Maybe Thomas wasn't the guy, but he'd made it clear he was angry that she'd walked away from him.

Ann rose from the couch. "Where are my manners? Would you like something to drink? I have a tea that has a calming effect. I can make some."

"I hate for you to go to the trouble. Your grandson should be calling any second." Beth stared at the phone as though willing it to ring.

A couple of minutes later, it did, and Beth shot to her feet. She covered the distance to the phone and started to reach for it, but Ann clasped the receiver and said, "Hello."

Her neighbor listened for a moment then hung up.

"Was that Colby?"

Ann nodded.

"What did he say?"

"It's okay for you to return home."

"Anything else?"

"No. I'll go with you."

Beth smiled. "You don't have to. I'll be fine." She walked toward the entry hall.

"Tell you what, I'll make you a cup of tea and bring it over. I promise my tea will help you. I can't even imagine how upset you are after having an intruder in your home."

Knowing Beth couldn't stop her neighbor from trying to help, she nodded. "I appreciate it." She hugged Ann. She and people like her were one of the reasons Beth had moved to Cimarron City.

Ann opened the front door. "Great. I'll be there soon."

The last thing Beth saw as the older woman closed her door was a big grin. The sight brought a calmness to Beth as she made her way back home.

She hurried toward her house, but she slowed as she approached the porch. Questions flooded her mind. How long had the intruder been inside? Why did he pick her place? Did the media coverage this past four weeks have anything to do with the break-in? What was he after?

* * *

With Duke at his side, Colby Parker stood at the front living room window and watched Beth Sherman pause and stare at her front door, frozen in place. He knew that look of fear on her face from his nine-years' experience as a police officer. He strode to the entrance to open the door.

Beth closed the space between them with slow, hesitant steps. "How bad is it inside?" She kept her gaze pinned on him as though she was scared to see what had happened to her "safe haven." Robbery victims often felt violated.

Worse than the vulnerability in her blue eyes was the fear in her expression. Since his fiancée died during a bank robbery years ago, he had devoted his life to protecting others. He hadn't been able to save Kelly. He should have been with her at the bank, but he'd slept through his alarm and arrived late. Maybe he could have saved her life.

"Not bad. I don't know if anything was taken. You might have scared him before he could do much. You'll have to go through and tell me if anything was stolen."

"He might have seen me." She peered into the living room. "He wasn't carrying anything, so if he took something it was small."

Colby followed Beth through her house as she checked different places. She released a long breath as she found her cell phone and laptop, picked them up to take with her, and set them on a table in her entry hall. He'd left two things that would have been easy to take.

When she closed her jewelry box in her bedroom, she turned toward him. "I can't think of anything that could have been taken."

"That's a good thing."

"Yes, but..." She walked back into the hallway. "What if it was him?" she asked in a quiet thoughtful tone.

"Who are you talking about?"

Beth's hands shook. She crossed her

arms against her chest. "Six months ago, I broke it off with my boyfriend, Thomas Carson. He didn't take it well. We lived in the same apartment complex, The Village, on the other side of Cimarron City. I moved here after my car was defaced and the tires were slashed. Nothing else has happened since that time until now."

"Was Thomas Carson the guy who left your house?"

"I don't know. The only thing I can say is that the intruder had a similar build as Thomas, but I couldn't tell you it was him."

"I've already called this in. Even though I just went off duty, I'll write up the report and also go by and interview Mr. Carson. What's his apartment number?"

"It's 289 on the second floor." Beth scanned her surroundings. "Can I come with you?"

"That's not a good idea. Let me do my job." Colby gestured toward the front door, open slightly. "It looks like the intruder picked your lock. You should install a more secure one and think about an alarm system too."

"I've been meaning to. Can you recommend a good lock and alarm system?"

"I'm not familiar with the companies in Cimarron City, but I'll ask some police officers I work with what they would recommend and let you know. It may take a couple of days."

The color faded from Beth's face.

He took a step toward her. "After I go see Thomas Carson, I can get you a good lock today and install it for you. Until then, why don't you stay with my grandma?"

"I hate to impose on Ann."

"You aren't." Nana pushed Beth's front door open wide and came inside, carrying a mug. "In fact, I insist you come to my house until this is cleared up." She handed the drink to Beth.

Her gaze flicked from his grandma to him. "Thank you. I appreciate you volunteering to put in a new lock. How about the back door?"

"You need a new one there, too. I'll replace both."

"That would be great." Beth sighed and

put the mug on a coaster nearby. "I'm going to gather a few items I don't want to lose."

She went through her house and came back carrying a bag full with her laptop, some pieces of jewelry, her cell phone, and a few clothing items. Beth picked up the tea, took a sip, and followed his grandma from her house.

Colby clicked the lock in place, closed her front door, then hurried to catch up with Beth and Nana. Duke trotted beside him. What he didn't tell Beth was that he had his dog sniff for bombs. Earlier today, there had been a bomb found in a backpack at a business a couple of miles from here. It had been disarmed, and no one was hurt, but so far there were no leads to who had left the bomb.

He didn't think there would be a bomb in Beth's house because the other one was a business, but he'd learned never to take anything for granted.

He strode to his truck and climbed inside after Duke settled on the backseat. He'd only returned to Cimarron City a couple of times since he'd left twelve years ago not long after Kelly's death. His grandmother had wanted him to move back since his college graduation in Florida. She finally wore him down, mostly because he missed Nana and his friends from his childhood, but he also needed to deal with the guilt he felt because of Kelly's murder. On one level in Tampa, he'd known he most likely couldn't have stopped what had happened in the bank, but a year-long relationship with Ashley hadn't lasted because he hadn't forgiven himself for not being there somehow and saving Kelly.

When he arrived at The Village, he exited his vehicle and signaled for Duke to come to him. Colby clipped on his dog's leash then headed for the apartment on the second floor. He pressed the button and heard the ring sound resonate through Carson's place. After waiting a minute, Colby pounded on the door.

A tenant left his residence down the hall, and Colby called out. "Sir, is this Thomas Carson's apartment?"

The guy nodded and continued toward

the stairs.

He must not be home. Colby would return tomorrow. In the meantime, he would look into the man. When he returned to his truck, he looked up at the building toward Carson's place. A slat on a blind over one of the windows in the man's apartment moved as if someone had been looking out at the parking lot.

Colby climbed into his truck then called into the station to find out what kind of vehicle Carson drove.

"A white SUV." The police officer also gave him the license plate number.

"Thanks."

He opened his door and stood on his running board to scan the parking lot for the vehicle. A white SUV was parked in the last row. Colby hopped down to the pavement and walked to it to check the license plate number. It was the same as the one registered to Thomas Carson. He felt the hood, and it was cool. But then with almost an hour passing since the break-in, it wouldn't be hot.

He still had questions for Carson, and

one way or another he would get some answers. Why didn't the guy come to the door a minute ago? Why was he probably peering out the window at him? What was the man hiding?

THREE

Beth paced back and forth in the kitchen while Ann checked the chili she insisted on making for Beth and Colby for dinner. It seemed like an eternity since he left to talk to Thomas.

"Honey, you're making me nervous. Sit. Relax. Let Colby handle this."

"It's been an hour." Each minute he'd been gone, she worried about his safety. It wasn't because she didn't think Colby could take care of himself. She'd discovered a very angry streak in Thomas in the last weeks they dated and the incidents that occurred after they'd broken up. Now she doubted her ability to read people correctly.

She'd always looked for the good in others.

Lord, what do I do?

Ann took the electric pot off its base, sat at the table, and poured more tea into their cups. "I'm a good listener. Is something else going on?"

"For a short time, I thought Thomas and I could have a lasting relationship. What Thomas has done makes me wonder if I can ever have one. My closest friends either have a husband or are in a serious relationship that will probably lead to marriage."

"I'm glad Thomas showed you who he is before you married him."

"Me too. Since Thomas, I've thrown myself into my job and our church. The past few months, I've often worked long hours, and I should have been at International Foods, Inc., instead of out jogging. My boss insisted I leave before five. I came home and took the opportunity to see if I'd like jogging."

Ann sipped her tea then set her cup on the placemat. "Do you like to jog? I hear it's a good form of exercise."

"Not high on my list. I'd prefer a bicycle—I think. I haven't been on one since I was a kid." Beth took a drink of the tea, savoring its taste, smooth and mellow. If she hadn't come home early, she might never have known someone had been in her house. That was scary. If only she could calm down and put the break-in behind her. Learn from it and make the necessary changes to her house and her ability to take care of herself. Maybe instead of riding a bicycle, she should take a self-defense class.

"Cimarron City has great bicycle paths throughout this town."

Before Beth could say anything, the sound of the front door opening and closing sent a shaft of fear down her body. She stiffened until she spied Colby with his dog come into the kitchen. The serious expression on his face drew her attention. "Did you talk with Thomas?"

He shook his head. "No one answered the door. I checked with a neighbor to make sure Carson still lived in the apartment." Colby rubbed the back of his neck. "When I left the building, I think someone in his place looked out a closed blind, but I'm not one hundred percent sure."

Most likely it was Thomas. He always checked out the peephole before opening a door and kept his blinds closed even during the day. "I think you're right."

"Where does he work?"

"Turner Construction."

"What are his work hours?"

"Usually eight to five." Beth glanced at the clock on the wall. Seven o'clock.

"Did he routinely go somewhere after work?"

"No, but he'd often go to the gym early in the morning before work. Do you think he might have something to do with what happened today?"

"He drives a white SUV, so yes. I want to talk to him."

"He does? He had a sports car when we dated."

Colby placed a sack on the counter nearby. "I have your locks. I'll change them after dinner." He drew in a deep breath and sat in a chair across from Beth. "It smells wonderful, Nana. I love your chili."

Ann pushed to her feet. "We'll eat as soon as I heat the bread."

"Can I help you set the table?" Beth stood.

After putting the rolls in the oven, her neighbor turned it on then glanced back at Beth, waving her hand. "We'll serve ourselves from here." Ann patted the stove. "I'm formal only on holidays when I have guests. Otherwise, I'm all for casual."

Colby leaned forward and whispered, "I tried to help when I first came but finally gave up when she ignored me and did what she wanted."

Beth chuckled. "That sounds like my mother."

"Do your parents live here?" His voice still held a soft tone as though they were having a private conversation.

"No, they recently moved to a small town in Texas called Bluebonnet."

"Did you grow up here?"

"No. I moved here when I got the job at IFI last year." Beth glanced toward Ann who put the plates on the counter next to the stove. She returned her gaze to Colby and stood. "If you didn't have your uniform on, I wouldn't be surprised if you told me you were a police officer. You're good at getting information from me." She smiled. "I don't normally tell a man I just met all I've told you in the past hours."

Laughing, Colby scooted his chair back and rose.

"Come and serve yourself. I'll bring the rolls to the table. I have water or iced tea." Ann gestured toward the pitcher of tea and the ice and water buttons on the refrigerator door.

When Beth settled in her seat at the table a few minutes later, the aroma of the chili aroused her hunger. She forgot she hadn't eaten lunch because she had worked through it, so she could leave the office a little early. What if she hadn't left her job early? It was possible she could have encountered the intruder in person in her house. The thought caused a shudder to run down her length.

"Let's pray," Ann said and bowed her

head. "Lord, thank You for this food. Please help Beth feel safe and my grandson to find the man who broke into her house. Blanket this street with peace. Amen."

When Beth lifted her gaze, she encountered Colby's eyes focused on her. For several seconds, she felt connected to him. It seemed impossible for her to drag her attention from him in order to enjoy the enticing food.

He looked away, breaking their bond, and picked up the bread basket. After taking a roll, he passed it to Beth. Their fingers touched, and she nearly dropped the container. She didn't and quickly passed it to Ann without taking anything from it.

As Ann took a piece of bread and set the basket on the table, she said, "I think you should stay here until your security system is in place. I have a spare bedroom."

"I appreciate the offer but—"

"I won't sleep a wink if you don't. Please, Beth, take my offer."

How could Beth say no—when she

didn't think she would sleep after what happened if she went back to her house without taking precautions?

"I think that's a good idea, Nana. I'd feel better too." Colby looked at Beth. "Then tomorrow when I go to work, I'll see what security company other police officers recommend."

"But I..." She wanted to say no because she hated to be indebted to others, but she couldn't. Ann was a friend trying to help her. "Okay. I'll need to get something to wear to work. I hope I can get a security company to come tomorrow."

Ann took a sip of her iced tea. "Don't worry if you can't get someone out right away. If you have to stay a few days, that's fine by me. I love having people around."

After helping Ann clean up the dinner dishes, Beth and Colby left to go to her house. As she approached her home with Colby, she couldn't stop her heartbeat from increasing its pace. The hairs on her nape tingled. Her gait slowed finally to a standstill.

"What's wrong?"

In the dark she scanned her surroundings. "I don't know. It just feels like someone is watching me."

He surveyed the area then held out his hand. "Give me the key."

Right after she did, he clasped her elbow and hurried her toward the front door. Once she was inside with Colby, he gave her key back to her.

"Did you see someone watching?" She fisted her hands at the thought he would verify her fear of a person surveilling her.

"No, but there were several places a person could hide. I'd rather play it safe."

"When I came here earlier to meet you, I didn't feel as scared, but this time it really hit me. I think it's because it's night, and when I looked around, I saw a lot of dark shadows that suddenly became a possible stalker watching me."

He moved closer. "I won't let anything happen to you. I'll be tracking down Thomas Carson tomorrow. If you want, I'll drive you to and from work. You have options. You aren't alone."

His last three words calmed the panic in

her. "I was scared after my tires were slit and my car was defaced, but I moved away from the apartment complex and nothing happened for months. Each day I felt safer."

"And you will again when we get your house more secured."

"How about a dog like Duke? Do you know of anyone who trains dogs for security or at least who has a breed that's protective?"

"I have a possible lead if he still lives here. I knew him in high school and back then he was working with dogs. But I'll also ask my fellow police officers. Do you want me to see what I can find?"

"Yes, please. I couldn't have an animal in the apartment building, but I can now."

"Okay. Let's get this done and go back to Nana's."

He started putting the new locks on the two doors while Beth packed a few more clothes and walked through the house again to make sure nothing was stolen. When Colby finished, he checked each window to make sure they were locked before he and Beth left her house. She kept her attention focused on what was before her. Her pace matched Colby's, and half a minute later, she was back inside Ann's home. She released a long breath. As a kid, she'd always been taught to be aware of her surroundings. She even took self-defense classes periodically with her mother. But since she'd been on her own now for six years, she'd let down her guard—even forgot some of the moves she'd learned as a teenager.

Before Colby stepped into the living room where Ann sat, she touched his arm. "Can you find a good instructor to teach me self-defense?"

He turned toward her. "Yes. I can help you with that."

She smiled. "Thanks. I appreciate that."

By the time she sat across from Ann, Beth felt as though a weight had been lifted from her shoulders. She wasn't alone.

* * *

The next morning, Beth pulled into the

parking lot at IFI earlier than usual because she didn't sleep well. Colby had said he would take her to her job if she wanted, but she needed to do it for herself. She couldn't let fear overpower her every move. She took the stairs up to the seventh floor where she worked. Two men stepped onto the elevator as Beth headed to her office. In the hallway, she passed Mollie Zoller an administrative assistant in the office next to hers. After Beth locked her purse into her lower drawer and walked back out into the corridor, she ran into two women she knew coming out of the breakroom.

Beth smiled and exchanged greetings then went into the breakroom to make a pot of coffee just the way her boss, Mr. Knight, liked it. As she waited, she tidied it up. Others on the floor often didn't clean up after themselves. She carried a handful of trash to the wastebasket in the corner. As she dropped the paper cups and napkins into the large can, she caught sight of a bag wedged between the refrigerator and the wall on the left side.

She covered the distance between her

and the backpack and reached out to yank it free. A few inches from her goal, she froze. The old bag didn't look familiar. Disquiet niggled at her mind. She backed away. There was something on the news this morning about a bomb in a backpack found at a business yesterday. As she stepped further away, her hand shook while she reached for her cell phone in her pocket.

FOUR

After stopping by The Village Apartments to see Thomas Carson before he went to work, Colby, with Duke at his side, again found no answer at Carson's front door. His white SUV still sat in the parking lot. He decided to retreat to his patrol vehicle and wait for Carson to head for his vehicle to go to work.

But when Colby left the building, he discovered the white SUV was gone. Had Carson somehow seen him approaching his apartment complex and escaped out an alternative entrance to avoid him?

The more Carson evaded him the more Colby thought the man had something to hide. When he climbed into his vehicle after securing Duke in the back, Colby received a message that there was another suspicious backpack found at IFI. He took down the needed information where the suspicious bag was discovered. That was where Beth worked, and she was the one who reported it. He could imagine what she was going through, especially after what happened yesterday.

Normally in an evacuation the elevators were shut down. In this case, he needed to arrive at the place where the backpack was found fast. "Make sure they hold an elevator on the ground level, so I can get to the seventh floor right away," Colby said to the dispatcher as he gripped the steering wheel so tightly that his knuckles whitened.

As he started the engine, he ground his teeth together. Not far from the company's headquarters, he would be able to respond to the call quickly.

When Colby arrived three minutes later at IFI, he was the first responder. He jumped from the patrol SUV and snapped the leash on Duke's collar. If there was a bomb in the backpack, his dog would be able to tell without moving it. He ran toward the building. An alarm was going off. People were flooding into the corridors from their offices on the first floor.

A security guard held an elevator open for Colby.

"I need to go straight up to the seventh floor."

"This elevator has an express button for the executive floor." The guard showed him what to press. "That's where you're going."

"Thanks. Help to move everyone out as fast as you can." After the guard left, Colby punched the button for the executive floor. As it ascended, Colby called Beth's cell phone to see if she was safely out of the building.

"Beth, where are you?"

"I'm outside the breakroom on the seventh floor."

"You should be evacuating the building along with the other employees."

"Where are you?"

"In the elevator coming to your floor. Which way do I go to get to the breakroom quickly?"

"I'm coming to the bank of elevators."

When the door slid open, the first thing Colby saw was Beth with creases of worry carved into her beautiful face. "Show me where to go. Then I want you to leave."

"You're going to stay around?" she asked as she rushed down a corridor.

"Yes, until the bomb squad arrives if Duke thinks it's a bomb." Colby entered a room with a mini kitchen, a table with eight chairs around it and a couch along a wall. He unhooked Duke's leash. "Find." As the dog made a beeline toward the refrigerator and sat, Colby followed. "Go now. The safest route out of here is to take the stairs on the other side of the building." He glanced back to make sure she obeyed.

* * *

Clutching her purse, Beth didn't want to leave Colby alone with a possible bomb only a couple of feet away from him. Still, she did as he said and took the staircase, jammed with other people making their way to the first floor.

Mollie descended with her. She leaned toward Beth and said in a voice louder than normal. "I just got a call from my husband. This isn't a fire, but there's a possible bomb in the building. Could it be the person who left one at the Prescott Rug Gallery yesterday?"

"A bomb?" a man in advertisement shouted right behind Beth.

The woman next to him screamed and tried to wedge herself between Mollie and Beth to move faster down the stairs. Her friend next to Beth stumbled and fell into the man in front of her. He turned quickly and saved Mollie from going forward.

Beth narrowed her eyes on the man from advertising and the woman behind her. "Quiet. We're almost to the first floor." She leaned toward them and whispered, "We don't want a stampede."

With the color draining from her face, the lady nodded.

When Beth was right above the second-floor landing on the stairs, a rush of people surged forward, grappling for a position in the line. Another person yelled, "Bomb."

The momentum to flee the building increased, and all Beth could do was pray and try to keep up with the panicked crowd. A man from the second floor knocked into her, slamming her against another employee. Beth fought to keep upright. Sweat ran down her face, and her breathing became shallow and fast.

By the time she reached the first floor, her progress almost came to a standstill while the mass funneled themselves through a one-door exit. When she emerged into the warm spring day, she hurried away from the building. She stopped in the parking lot and swept around to look at IFI. She struggled to slow her fast heartbeat while she took in deep breaths.

No sight of Colby.

A police officer stood nearby shouting to the crowd, "Get away from here. Stay behind the barricades." He gestured toward the barriers across the road and at the end of the street.

As Beth headed for the security line,

she kept looking over her shoulder at the main doors. Where was Colby? Was the bomb squad here yet? What if it went off with him still inside?

She scanned the area and spied the bomb squad's van. She blew out a long sigh. Hopefully, that meant Colby would be outside soon. But the minutes ticked by, and there wasn't a glimpse of him coming or going from the building nor among the police spread out to keep the people away from IFI.

Nibbling on her thumbnail, Beth focused her stare on the main entrance. When the bomb squad came out with a blast container, she kept her attention on the door. Still no Colby. As a few of the people left, she began pacing. Her boss was talking with the bomb squad commander. The man passed a megaphone to Mr. Knight as another police officer and a dog went into the building.

"We're shutting down the building for the day. The police will be going through IFI from top to bottom. Please go home, and you'll receive a call to tell you when it's okay to return to work."

Reporters, standing not far from Beth, shouted questions about the incident.

"Is this the same guy who left a bomb yesterday?" one yelled above several others.

"We can't confirm this is the same person at this time," a police captain said into a microphone thrust close to his face. "We'll have a press conference when we have more information. Right now, we need you to disperse. For safety reasons, leave the scene."

Beth didn't want to leave. What if there was more than one bomb? Could Colby and the others find them before they went off?

Lord, please keep him and the other police officers safe.

Beth followed the crowd heading for their cars. At least she could call some security firms for suggestions on what she should have at her house. When she arrived on her street, she thought of going to her home to make the calls, but she drove past her place and parked in Ann's driveway. Glancing two doors down sent a shiver up her spine. She couldn't go to her home right now.

Before Beth could ring the doorbell, Ann appeared and stepped back to let Beth into her house.

The older woman took a hard look at Beth. "I saw you pull into the driveway from the living room window. What's wrong?"

"I found a bomb left at IFI." Beth told Ann the details as she walked into the kitchen. "After this morning and yesterday, I didn't want to be alone."

Ann hugged Beth. "Colby will let us know what's going on when he can. I have tea. Would you like a cup?"

"Yes, thank you. Could I have the soothing and calming tea you gave me previously? I need that. It's only nine, and I'm already tied up into knots."

"Child, I would be too if I found a bomb."

Beth sat in a chair, her legs too shaky to keep standing.

Ann put the teapot on then took two mugs from the cabinet. When she brought a cup and set it down in front of Beth on a placemat, she laid her hand on Beth's shoulder. "You aren't alone in this. First and foremost, the Lord is looking out for you. You're one of His children. Then there's me and my grandson." She took a seat in a chair catty-cornered from Beth and added, "After you left this morning, I called a few friends who've recently gotten a security system. I wrote down their information and who they recommend doing it."

Beth smiled. "Ann, thanks. You're a dear friend." She drank a sip of the tea. "I'll call those security firms and decide what I want and can afford."

It would give her something to do while she waited for Colby to let her know what happened at IFI after she left. From the reaction of the police at the scene, there must have been a bomb in the backpack. She shuddered at the thought of how close she'd been to it.

Why would someone plant a bomb at IFI?

* * *

Colby pulled into his grandmother's driveway and parked next to Beth's car. Both he and Duke needed a break after spending intense hours searching several floors of the IFI building while other police officers and canine partners, some from other parts of Oklahoma, took the rest of the company. The only bomb found was on the seventh floor where Beth discovered it. Why there? What connected IFI and the Prescott Rug Gallery?

Beth opened the front door before he had a chance to insert his key. Her cheeks were flushed as though she had hurried into the entry hall, but for a long moment, he couldn't take his eyes off her beautiful face framed by a mass of blond hair. What drove him earlier today was the thought what would have happened if Beth hadn't found the backpack.

Her focus remained locked with his. "Did you find any more bombs? Or find the person who's doing this?"

"No to both questions." He entered the

house as Beth stepped to the side. The same fear he saw yesterday in her blue eyes lurked there again, and all he wanted to do was wipe that look away. He unhooked Duke's leash, put it on the small table nearby, then grasped her hands. "But I'm hoping you can help me."

"Me. How?"

"I need to interview you about finding the backpack. You may have seen something that might help us."

"Other than the backpack, what else?"

Colby strolled into the living room. "Where's Nana?"

"At church. She should be home in an hour or so. Velma came by and picked her up. I think she needed to keep busy, so she didn't think about you still being at IFI. She wanted me to go too, but I wouldn't have been any help."

While Beth sat at one end of the couch, he took a seat at the other end. "After going through security, what did you do?"

"I took the stairs up to the seventh floor. I've been doing that since I worked there as a form of exercise. I didn't see anyone in the stairwell with a backpack. Carol Dunkin and Janet Ripley were in front of me until they exited at the sixth floor where they work."

"When you got to the seventh floor, who did you see?"

"A few people on the seventh floor when I first came in. There were two men at the elevator, but the only person I saw that I know is Mollie Zoller, who works in the office next to mine. There are four hundred employees in the building. She might know who the men were. They were both in their thirties, I think, but I've only seen one of them before at IFI. They took the elevator down as I passed them."

Colby wrote down Mollie's name on his pad to follow up after his interview with Beth. "Did you go right to the breakroom?"

"No. I always go to my office, put my purse away, and make sure there isn't anything that has to be done right away. Then I make the coffee for Mr. Knight, myself, and anyone else who wants some." She grinned. "Making coffee is one of my talents. At lunch, I make another pot at the request of my fellow workers on the floor."

"When you went to the breakroom, was there anyone in there?"

She nodded. "Two people were leaving when I came around the corner to go to the breakroom. They work on my floor. April Dawson and Kay Smith."

Colby put those names in his notebook too. "It might be a longshot, but the security tape of that hallway was down. I don't believe that was a coincidence."

"I thought we had a good security system in place."

"The bomb didn't have any metal that would be discovered by the metal detector used at IFI. The type of bomb was the same as the one found at the store yesterday."

"So, it's possible the person who left the bombs works at IFI?"

"Yes, or some kind of tie to the company."

She clasped her hands together tightly. "How many minutes until it would have gone off?"

"Thirty minutes. It was more powerful

than the one at the store. A different color but the same type of backpack. Do you know if the breakroom is used that early in the morning?"

"Occasionally people eat something for breakfast that they picked up on the way to work or some will put a lunch they brought in the refrigerator. But most of the time the breakroom isn't used until around nine-thirty."

"And you make your coffee at about eight-thirty every morning?"

"Yes, depending on Mr. Knight's schedule. Sometimes a little earlier or later."

"How often do the two people that left there this morning use the breakroom at that time?"

"Not often, that I know of. This morning I was earlier than usual because I didn't sleep well last night. I went to make coffee a little before eight."

He hadn't slept much either. Since Beth told him the night before she would drive her car to IFI, he'd left for work before seven and had wanted to connect with

Carson.

"Oh, no!" Beth widened her eyes and covered her mouth with her hand.

"What's wrong?"

"If I hadn't come to the breakroom early, the bomb would have gone off before the bomb squad arrived."

He'd known that but hadn't wanted Beth to realize how close she'd come to being killed. She already had a problem with someone breaking into her house. He scooted toward her and took her trembling hand. "You saved a lot of people. Focus on that."

"How about the cameras on each floor?"

"The one to that hall malfunctioned for a while early this morning. That's when the bomb must have been planted and set to go off when everyone was at work. We will comb through all the video we have of the building, but that will take a while." And the people in the building at that time were being investigated. He would be kept busy as long as this perpetrator remained at large. "There were two K-9 teams with dogs that specialized in finding bombs at first. Then later a few teams from around the state came and helped."

"I can't believe the bomber could be someone who works at IFI. What if he tries to do it again?"

"My commander told me that IFI is bringing in several bomb-sniffing dogs. That way the building will be safe as they tighten their security procedures. Duke and I and the other K-9 team will be available for any other sighting in Cimarron City."

"What does the Prescott Rug Gallery and IFI have in common that a bomber would target them?"

"Good question. If we could figure that out, we could close in on the person responsible. I hope there's a connection. If this is random, it may be harder to discover and solve who's behind it."

"Random? I hate the idea of someone at IFI being responsible, but random is worse. The list of suspects is a hundred percent more." Lines of worry crinkled her forehead.

Before he could say anything else, his cell phone rang, and he quickly answered it. "A backpack was found at Cimarron City Bank. You're two minutes away," the police dispatcher said.

FIVE

An hour later, Colby left the bank with Duke by his side, relieved that the backpack belonged to a customer who left it behind when he'd forgotten something in his car and went to retrieve it. A woman who came into the lobby saw it unattended and called the police.

He drove to The Village Apartments to see if Carson's SUV was in the parking lot. It wasn't. He continued to Turner Construction, hoping another bomb scare didn't detour him again. He couldn't shake the feeling the man was trying to avoid him as though he was guilty of breaking into Beth's house.

At Carson's work, he approached the receptionist. "I'm here to talk to Thomas Carson."

"He called in sick today."

"Did he call in sick yesterday?"

"I don't know. I wasn't on this desk."

"Who's his supervisor?"

"Alex Wilson. He's out in the warehouse behind this building." The woman pointed in that direction.

"Thank you." Near the receptionist's desk, Colby spied an exit door at the end of a hallway and headed down it. The warehouse was only twenty feet from the main building. When he entered, he saw a man around forty years old wearing a hardhat talking to a younger guy. Colby approached him.

When the older man finished, he turned toward Colby who approached him. "Can I help you," he looked at Colby's name plate under his badge, "Officer Parker?"

"Yes. I'm looking for Thomas Carson. Are you his supervisor?"

"I am. Is there a problem?"

"Not at this time. I understand he's sick

today. Was he here yesterday?"

"No."

"Do you know what's wrong with him?"

"No, not exactly, but he was coughing when he called to let me know he wouldn't be in on Monday. I've had several men out these past couple of weeks with the flu. He might have caught that."

"What does he do here?"

"He's the assistant manager of the warehouse."

"Thank you." As Colby left, he scanned the place filled with work-site supplies.

After leaving Turner Construction, he drove again to The Village Apartments and finally spotted the SUV in the parking lot. He stopped, strode into the building with Duke, and rang the bell. Again, no answer.

The urge to slam his fist against the wall swamped him for a few seconds. Colby sucked in a calming breath and left. He drove down the street and pulled over. After he climbed from his patrol vehicle with Duke, he walked back to the parking lot, near Carson's SUV. He found a place that afforded a side view of Carson's apartment. Colby realized he might not be able to stake out the vehicle for long. But this man was going to a lot of trouble to stay away from him. If he wasn't responsible for the break-in at Beth's, then why was he avoiding talking to the police?

Fifteen minutes later, Colby got the opportunity to find out. A man exited his apartment building by the back entrance. Colby was pretty sure that guy was Beth's ex-boyfriend but checked Carson's driver's license photo to make sure it was him. As Carson made his way toward his SUV, he kept looking around and using other vehicles to hide himself. When Carson reached the driver's side of his car, Colby, with Duke at his side, sneaked from behind the bush he'd used to hide. He quickened his pace toward Carson, who glanced up and saw Colby. The man stiffened while fumbling for his key fob in his pocket.

"Thomas Carson, I have some questions for you."

Color drained from his pale face. "I don't have the time right now. I have to get to work."

"We can talk here or down at the station. Which do you want?"

Carson blew out a loud breath and leaned against the driver's side door with his arms crossed over his chest. "Make it short. I don't want to lose my job."

"I know you've called in sick for the past two days, but you appear all right to me. Where were you yesterday from four to six in the afternoon? You weren't at work according to your boss. I came to talk to you, and no one answered the door, so where were you?"

Carson dropped his head. "I took some medicine that knocked me out. I vaguely recall hearing the doorbell, but I was so groggy I didn't get up to answer the door." When he looked up, he asked, "Why are you wanting to know where I was yesterday?"

"A SUV similar to yours was sighted leaving a scene of a crime." So far, looking at a couple of neighbors' outside security camera footage hadn't produced the license plate number, only a partial glimpse of a white SUV on one of them.

"It wasn't mine. I was asleep as I said." The man frowned and climbed into his vehicle. "What crime scene?"

"A break-in."

Carson harrumphed. "I make good money. I don't need to steal."

Before Colby could reply, Beth's ex-boyfriend drove away.

As Colby made his way back to his patrol vehicle, he received another message of a suspicious backpack in the park. He jogged to his vehicle and put on his siren as he headed for the children's playground.

* * *

Late afternoon, Ann stood next to Beth on her porch, waiting for Jack Robison from Safe Security. Colby had called and told Beth about the company's reasonable prices and recommendations by several other cops. A white van with the name of the business plastered on its sides pulled in and parked.

Beth sighed. "In the middle of all the

chaos today, I can't believe Colby had time to ask about a good security firm and also get someone to come out and take a look at my house. I'll feel so much better when I have a good system in place."

Ann clasped her arm. "You don't have to leave my home until you feel safe. I love having you as a guest."

"That means so much to me." Beth stepped forward when the man approached her house. "Thanks for coming on short notice. I had a break-in yesterday, and the police officer suggested getting some security. My locks have been replaced. What else should I do?"

"Let me take a look. We have several plans."

Beth entered her place with Ann right behind her.

"Your front door is made of solid wood. That's good. Do you have a back one?"

Beth nodded. "And one to the garage."

Mr. Robison walked from one room to the next. When they returned to the living room, Beth hoped she could afford a good security system. Her budget was tight.

KIDNAPPED

Moving into this home had stretched her budget.

"We can put alarms on all the doors and even the windows. You'll control turning the alarm on and off from inside on the panel and outside from an app on your cell phone. The alarm can be on while you're here or away. I can place a couple of motion detectors in key places, security lights outside, and cameras where you want."

When Mr. Robison finished showing her what he could do, Beth agreed to a basic program with a few lights and cameras outside. They would come out and put it in on Monday—six days from today.

"What time of day on Monday?" Beth asked, realizing she would have to make arrangements to take a few hours off to be at the house when they put in the security system.

"Three o'clock. Two of my men will come then." Mr. Robison headed for the entry hall. "If you have any questions about how it will work, they'll be able to answer you."

"Thanks, Mr. Robison." Beth shut the front door.

Ann grinned. "You're gonna have a safe home, and I'm gonna have you as my guest for six days." She leaned toward Beth. "You can help me persuade Colby to go to church with us this Sunday. He used to go, but he stopped attending after Kelly was killed. It broke my heart. Instead of turning away, he should have been turning toward the Lord."

"Who was Kelly?"

"She was his fiancée I told you about. She was murdered in a robbery, and Colby blames himself. He was supposed to meet her at the bank to apply for a loan on a small home, but he overslept and ran late. He blames himself for her death. Somehow, he felt if he'd been there, he could have prevented it."

"That's so sad. It wasn't his fault. It was the man who killed her."

"I know that, and you do. But Colby wasn't able to get past it. He left here, but after years, he's finally returned to Cimarron City. I think he's ready to move on. At least I hope so."

"So do I. We can't really control what others do. He didn't know about the robber inside the bank. Was he a police officer at the time?"

"No. He was a college freshman. The incident led him to becoming a police officer."

"I'm going to get some more clothes to cover the next five days." Beth started for her bedroom.

As she packed a small suitcase, she thought about the many times she and her parents had moved when she was child. She wanted to stay in Cimarron City longer than a year. She hoped she would be able to call it home. Putting down roots and having friends she could depend on were important to her. As a child, she'd come close to it, and then her dad would get a new job and they left.

As she exited her bedroom, she realized that in a couple of weeks she would have lived in Cimarron City for fifteen months. She smiled. She was determined that would turn into fifteen years. She wouldn't let Thomas or whoever invaded her home to force her to leave.

"Ready? It's getting late." Ann walked toward the entry hall. "I need to start dinner, one I can throw together fast. Colby most likely skipped lunch again today and will be starving."

"I'll help you. What are you making?"

"Nothing fancy. Homemade macaroni and cheese and grilled steaks with a salad to balance out the meal."

"I may not cook a lot, but I know how to make a salad. Let me do that."

Ann unlocked her front door and moved into her house. "Sounds good to me, and we'll have Colby fire up the grill and take care of the T-bone steaks. In fact, it's a gorgeous day. We should eat outside."

An hour later, after Colby arrived home and showered, he entered the kitchen with Duke right behind him. "I'm ready to do my part with this meal."

Beth's gaze took in his refreshed appearance. His brown hair was still damp. He looked totally different in his jeans and T-shirt than when he wore his police uniform. She opened the refrigerator, pulled out the platter of steaks, and handed them to Colby.

Duke barked.

Colby laughed. "My dog is going to be happy after we eat our steaks. He loves the bones. He's just reminding me not to forget him." He headed outside.

The second the door closed behind him, Ann asked, "Can you take the plates, glasses, and utensils outside? We'll also use the placemats from the kitchen table."

"This is a great idea. It's a beautiful spring day."

"You don't need to come back inside. I'll bring the salad and macaroni and cheese out when the steaks are cooked."

Beth lowered her head and grinned. Ann was known to play matchmaker at church. Now she was trying it in her home. She appreciated her friend's efforts, but after dating Thomas, she was leery about her judgment when it came to whom she should go out with.

Since Thomas, she hadn't dated anyone. By the time she left him, she'd realized he was a narcissist. The signs had been there. At first, he'd been charming and persuasive. But with time, another side had come out: a person who felt entitled to what he wanted, always breaking the rules. To him they didn't apply, and when he didn't get his way, he threw a tantrum like a young child.

When she began setting the picnic table on the back deck, Colby looked up at her. "How did the meeting go with the security company?"

"I'm getting a system next Monday."

"Will it make you feel better?"

"I hope so. I think it will, but until I move back into my house, I won't know for sure." Beth sat in a comfortable patio chair.

After Colby flipped the steaks, he took a seat near her. "I'm still looking into Thomas Carson. I finally talked to him today. He knows I'm on a break-in case."

"I'm surprised you had time to do anything. Besides my call about a backpack, I heard there were two other ones—thankfully, all false."

"Duke and I are the best team to assess

a possible bombing situation quickly. Duke's a special dog. He can detect a bomb and its location whereas a person has to hunt for the actual bomb if it's hidden. But he can also track a person using their particular scent. If someone moves through a crowd with a bomb, Duke can pick up the scent and follow the trail."

"Then I have a feeling you'll continue to be busy until the person responsible is caught."

"I hope he can be caught before one goes off. We've been lucky so far. If you hadn't been early today, a lot of people could have died. We had time to keep it from exploding at IFI. Letting the public know about the backpack bomber will, hopefully, help us stop him before one detonates, even if I have to run from one sighting to another."

"It's going to be hard to show up tomorrow at work."

Colby stood, covered the distance to the grill, and started putting the meat on a platter. "After today, IFI and other companies are looking at security measures and implementing them ASAP. We went through the building and didn't find any other bombs."

Ann came outside with the salad.

Beth hopped up. "I'll get the rest." She hurried inside before Ann insisted that she could bring out the tea and casserole dish.

When Beth returned with the macaroni and cheese and the tea on a tray, she sat next to Ann with Colby across from Beth. Ann blessed the food then passed the salad bowl.

Beth relaxed for the first time in the past twenty-four hours and enjoyed the meal. She usually ate alone and hadn't realized how much she'd missed not having company when eating. As she listened to Ann trying to convince Colby to go to church with them on Sunday, Beth's thoughts drifted back to yesterday when the man ran out of her house. Something bothered her, but she couldn't put her finger on what it was.

"Beth, do you want dessert?"

Ann's question penetrated her musing. Beth blinked several times and focused on her friend. "No, I'm watching my weight since I'm giving up jogging."

Ann smiled. "I'm glad you were jogging yesterday and weren't there when that man invaded your home."

Thinking about that time stirred a question in her mind. "I've been wondering something about the guy. He left my house, but not because he saw me. I've been thinking about that. At first, I thought he might have seen me. But now, I don't think he knew I was there. So why didn't he steal from me? Why else would he be inside?"

SIX

Other than sleeping five hours last night, Colby hadn't stopped since he opened the door to find Beth needing help. "Maybe we should go back to your house after dinner. It's possible with all that happened yesterday, you overlooked something."

Beth ran her fingers through her long blond hair. "I'm probably worrying about nothing. I should be happy they didn't take anything."

"I know how upset you were. You wouldn't be the first person not to find everything that was taken when robbed."

"Then, yes. I want to recheck my house

if you have the time tonight."

"We will." Colby took his steak bone and tossed it out into the yard. "Enjoy, Duke."

His dog raced toward his prize. Beth grinned while watching Duke attack his bone. "I think he likes his treat."

Colby rose and gathered some of the dishes. "We'll clean up, Nana, then go to Beth's."

"No, I'll take care of the dishes. Then when you two come back, we'll enjoy a slice of my peach cobbler."

"But—"

His grandmother pushed to her feet. "Colby, not one word of protest. I'm cleaning up. End of story."

He threw up his hands, palms outward. "I was only trying to help."

"You put in a long, tiring day. I enjoy taking care of you." She took the plates and utensils near her and walked toward the back entrance.

Beth scooped up the salad bowl and hurried to the door to hold it open for his grandma.

Colby took the rest of the dishes to the sink "Duke, come."

After clearing the table, he and Beth left for her house. Duke trotted between them.

"Your dog is well behaved. He hadn't quite finished his bone, and yet he came to you when you called him."

"We've been partners for several years. I volunteered for a national program that supplies canine teams to police departments. The training was extensive for both me and Duke."

"How did you end up here?"

"The opportunity to return to Cimarron City came up, and I decided it was time I came home. With my dad and mom living in Arizona, I felt a family member should be here for my grandmother if she ever needed someone." That and he had to deal with Kelly's death, or he would never be able to move on.

"Both sets of my grandparents are dead. My family is very small. No aunts or uncles either," Beth offered.

"You're right. That is small. My family's a little bit bigger than that. They just don't live here anymore except for a second cousin who's been feuding with Nana for years."

"Feuding?" Beth unlocked her front door and stepped inside.

"When my great-grandmother died, Nana received furniture my cousin thought was hers. But the will left them to Nana. They haven't talked with each other since that day in the lawyer's office."

"Do you and your cousin get along?"

"We're on talking terms. She works for the police department. Marie Adams is the secretary for the chief of police."

"I know Marie. She attends the same church that Ann and I attend."

"Have they ever talked to each other?"

Beth cocked her head to the right and stared at the wall past Colby's shoulder. "No. Not that I've ever seen. Marie started working in the church nursery on Sunday. I didn't realize she was the police chief's secretary."

"I don't think she's been for long. We briefly talked my first day on the job after I spoke with the chief."

"Does Ann know Marie is working for the chief of police?"

"No. Not long after I arrived at Nana's, a certain lady came to the door and claimed her house had been broken into."

"I'm starting in my bedroom."

"Do you want me to come with you?"

She paused in the entry hall and turned toward him. "Yes. I don't want to be alone."

Colby cut the distance between them. "Duke, guard."

Beth started with her dresser. "So until last weekend, you hadn't been back to Cimarron City in years?"

"No, I returned a few times when I heard something in Nana's voice."

Beth moved to her closet after checking all her drawers. "Maybe we should try to bring Marie and Ann together. Family is important. I wish I had more. I always wanted to have a little sister or even a brother. But I never got that."

Colby came to the entrance into the walk-in closet and leaned his upper arm against the doorjamb. "Neither did I. After me, Mom could never have another child."

"In my case, my parents didn't want any more children. I heard them talking one night when I was seven. I remember going back to my bed and crying myself to sleep. We'd just moved to a new place, and I felt so alone. I hated moving a lot."

The quiver in her voice cut through him. He'd been an only child and understood what she'd felt as a child. He'd experienced loneliness at times too, although he never moved around like she had. He'd lived nineteen years in Cimarron City and twelve in Tampa. Those were the only places he'd called home.

When she looked up from going through a box on the floor, their gazes linked together. Her eyes shone with tears she tried to keep inside. She swiped her hand across her cheek. "I think everything is crashing down on me. First the break-in and then today the bomb."

Colby knelt in front of her and clasped her hands. "We don't have to do this tonight."

She tried to smile, but it faltered almost

immediately. "We're here. I need to finish."

"Is there something I can help you with?"

"Yes. Stay and help me take my mind off the reason I'm sitting on my closet floor going through boxes."

Colby settled on the carpeted floor next to her, not sure he was the guy to take her mind off what was going on. She'd been involved in two incidents. Each one alone would rattle a person. Two in less than a day was overwhelming. "I'll help you make this house as safe as possible. You mentioned getting a dog. I think you should consider it."

"A puppy?"

"I know someone who might be able to help. He has one that's eleven months old that can be trained to protect you. I can help you with that too."

She turned her head and looked him straight in the eye. "Am I overreacting to what happened?"

"No," he said, still seeing her shell-shocked expression. "Although you weren't physically in the house when that man bridged your sanctuary, it makes you feel assaulted. I've dealt with a lot of people who had their house invaded."

"Then I come back to why did he do it." She pointed toward her bedroom. "I haven't found anything in here. This is where I keep most of my valuables, which aren't a lot. The TV and computer were still in the living room. Unless he put something small in his pocket, the guy didn't have anything of mine. So why did he come?"

If Carson was the guy, it was possible he had something else on his mind. "Are you finished in here?"

"In the bedroom, yes."

"Do you mind if I take a look around?"

She furrowed her brow. "No."

Colby made a tour of the bedroom. "You recognize all your items in here as yours."

Beth scanned the room. "Everything is…" Her frown deepened, and she stepped forward and picked up her clock. "I think this looks—"

"What?"

"New. Mine is several years old. This

one doesn't look quite right."

He held out his hand. "May I see it?" He checked it and found why the intruder must have come to the house. "It has a camera in it."

"In my bedroom!" She sank onto her bed, crossed her arms, and shook her head.

"I'll go through the rest of the house while you continue checking to see if anything valuable was taken. I'll leave Duke here while I run to my truck to get my gloves and evidence bags." His gut was telling him there would be other cameras and, most likely, Carson was involved. Was yesterday the first day the cameras had been placed or had they been placed earlier? Could it be that the feed hadn't come through, so the intruder returned to fix it?

* * *

An hour later Beth sat in her living room, panning her surroundings as though hundreds of eyes were boring into her. Now she knew what prompted the break-in, but what she'd discovered made her feel even worse. It had to be Thomas. The idea churned her stomach. She'd thought she'd escaped him, but she hadn't. He'd been spying on her probably the whole time.

She leaned against the sofa's back cushion and closed her eyes. She didn't see how she could feel safe in this house ever again.

What do I do, Lord? Leave Cimarron City—a place where she'd found a job she loved, friends, and a church? Sell her house and move to another place here? Would that even be enough? Why didn't she realize the type of person Thomas was—a narcissist? What tells had Thomas given to clue her to his real personality? The first few months, he'd made her feel special, then he changed as though he'd gotten bored with her.

The sound of footsteps drifted to her. She bolted straight up on the couch, flipping her long blond hair over her shoulders. "Another one?" Exhaustion weaved its way through her.

"Yeah. The other smoke alarm has a camera too. I think it's time we leave. It's been a long day for both of us. I'm afraid I'll be going from one backpack sighting to the next tomorrow. When I'm off duty, I'll return with a bug detector to make sure I have them all." He put the smoke alarm in an evidence bag on the coffee table with the other devices that had cameras. After removing his gloves, he held his hand out to her.

She clasped his fingers and stood with a little help from Colby. "I still can't believe Thomas would do this to me. I know we parted on bad terms, but to bug my house, that's…" A shudder snaked down her spine. She couldn't find the words to complete her sentence. Nor could she dismiss the repugnant feeling in the pit of her stomach.

"An invasion?"

She nodded. "Everything is catching up with me."

"I'm going to get help with this case." He scooped up the bags of evidence. "I'll be caught up in the search for the person leaving the bombs until we find him. I was put on the task force this afternoon. What we found tonight makes this more than a break-in with nothing taken. I have a high school friend who's a detective on the force. I'm going to bring him in on your case."

"I want you to find whoever left the bomb at IFI. My friends from work and I could have been killed today. Finding the bomber is much more important." Beth left her house last and locked the door.

"If he keeps it up, one of them will go off. That's what I'm afraid of." Colby's jaw set in a hard line.

"I agree. The unknown is scary."

Colby reached his grandmother's house. "I need to take these evidence bags down to headquarters. I won't be gone for long. Duke, guard."

When Beth entered Ann's house, his dog followed her.

His grandma came into the entry hall from the living room. She glanced at the bags Colby clutched in his fists. "What are those?"

"Evidence from Beth's house. I'll be

right back."

When he left, Beth put her arm around Ann and headed into the kitchen. "I could use some of your calming tea right now."

After fixing the tea and handing Beth a mug of the soothing liquid, Ann sat across from her at the kitchen table. "What was in those bags?"

Beth gave her a list of what Colby took to the police station.

"Oh, Beth, I'm so sorry."

She took a long sip of her tea. "I don't know that I would have found those devices if it hadn't been for Colby. I can't believe someone, even Thomas, would do that. I know he wasn't happy with me for breaking up with him. It makes me question my ability to read people correctly. At first Thomas swept me off my feet. We dated for three months with little that concerned me. It was the last two months that brought out his disturbing behavior—his possessive and seething angry personality."

"Some people are good at hiding their real personality behind a mask. You've always looked at the good side of a person. I've seen it firsthand at church. When you joined not long after you came to Cimarron City, you jumped right in to help wherever it was needed. Don't forget you have people who care about you and will help you."

Beth smiled. "I appreciate you, Ann. You always know how to make a person feel better."

By the time Beth finished a second cup of tea, Colby returned and came into the kitchen. He looked as tired as she felt.

"The bags have been logged in, and I brought Detective Nick Davidson in on the case. He'll let me know if he finds anything. He wants to talk to you tomorrow. I gave him your cell phone number. He'll call you and set up a time to meet." He gave Beth the detective's number, and she added it to her contacts.

"Thanks. I appreciate your help." Beth rose, walked to the dishwasher, and put the mug on the top rack. "I'm going to bed." She leaned around Colby to say, "Ann, I appreciate the tea and your friendship."

In her bedroom, Beth sank onto the mattress, gripping part of the covers on both sides of her. She thought of where the cameras had been found, especially the one in her bedroom and another in her bathroom. When had the person placed those cameras in her house? When she first moved in, yesterday, or somewhere between those times? Where was the video footage? What did it show and why did Thomas do it?

SEVEN

Beth exited her car in the IFI parking lot next to the seven-floor building. Only a fifth of the employees were returning today because the executives needed more time to make sure there wasn't a repeat of yesterday. The security would be tested during the day. Each department would meet for suggestions.

As she approached the main entrance, the only one open today, two-armed security guards flanked the double doors. Everyone had to have their company badge hanging from a lanyard. As she passed the guards, they zeroed in on her ID even though she knew both of them. Inside, every bag, purse, backpack, and briefcase were searched physically until the more sensitive screening machines arrived later that day.

When she entered her office, her boss, Mr. Knight, came to the doorway. "How are you doing?"

He'd called her several times yesterday in between intense meetings with the other top executives. "Okay. When I was going through security, I kept thinking about how sad it is that we have to do this to try and keep us safe from bad people."

He nodded. "That's what my wife and I talked about last night. She told me you had a break-in on Monday."

"How did Sadie find out?"

"Ann Maxwell. Can I help in anyway? What have the police discovered?"

"Not much. Thankfully nothing was taken."

"That's odd."

She had a lot of respect for Mr. Knight, but she didn't want to tell him what Colby and she'd found in her house last night. And she would make sure Ann didn't say anything to anyone, especially Sadie. The more she'd thought about the video footage that might have been captured on the cameras, the more she wanted to hide. What an invasion of her privacy! What if a shot of her taking a shower had been uploaded to the Internet? Her stomach roiled. The heat of a flush scored her face. "The intruder was interrupted when I came home from jogging."

"Take a few days off. You've had not one traumatic experience but two."

"Work will take my mind off them. I would like to take Monday afternoon off, though. I'm getting a security system put in that day." Ann had volunteered to oversee the installment, but Beth felt she needed to be there and make sure she knew every aspect of what she was purchasing.

"I understand and yes to Monday afternoon." He started to turn back into his office but paused. "I'd like you at a meeting with the president and the senior executives to take notes of anything I'll need to remember or address. It's in the boardroom in an hour."

Beth followed her usual routine, putting her purse in her bottom drawer then walking out into the hallway toward the breakroom. She did it so automatically every morning, but when she entered the breakroom, she came to a halt as though she'd been flash-frozen. Her gaze riveted to the spot where the bomb in the backpack had been yesterday with only thirty minutes on the timer. She crept toward the refrigerator and peeked around the corner.

No backpack this time.

She leaned into the fridge, clutching it. If she'd been able to sleep Monday night, she and the others would have died or been injured. Something bad like the break-in had ended up saving her life yesterday. God was watching over her.

Thank You, Lord. I won't disappoint You.

She moved to the counter and prepared the coffee. Both of the persons behind the cameras in her house and the placing of the bombs in Cimarron City would be caught.

As she poured the coffee into Mr. Knight's mug then hers, her cell phone rang. She noticed it was from Colby and quickly answered it. "Hi, how's this morning going so far?"

"Quiet, but then it's only been two hours since I reported to work. I did talk with Nick about your case. He's paying Carson a visit today after he gets the evidence report from the items in your house."

"Thanks for letting me know what's going on."

"I drove by The Village Apartments and noticed Carson's SUV was gone, so I told Nick he's probably at work. Actually, I'm on my way to Turner Construction to see if his vehicle is there."

"I thought you turned it over to your friend."

Colby chuckled. "I did, although I told him I would help when I had the time. I can't walk away from—" A voice in the background cut into their conversation.

It sounded like a call came in from the police station, but other than the words, "there's been," the rest was muffled as though Colby must have put his hand over the microphone on his cell.

"Beth, I've got to go," Colby said.

Before she could reply, the call went dead.

Please, not another bomb threat.

* * *

Colby turned on his siren and stepped on his accelerator. What he'd hoped would never happen occurred minutes ago. A bomb went off in a grocery store on the other side of Cimarron City.

When he reached the bombsite, he parked in the front parking lot. Colby, with Duke on a leash, hurried to the command center nearby and approached Captain McHenry who was in charge.

The captain waved his hand toward the people behind the barricades. "Walk through the gathering crowd. The bomber may be there watching the effects of his work."

Colby weaved through the people

across the four-lane street. As he and Duke progressed from the left to the right of the large gathering, he locked gazes with a man, his shoulders hunched forward, his hoodie covering a lot of his face. The guy swung around and shoved the person next to him and then ran. Colby pressed his way through the crowd in the direction of the fleeing man. As the runner disappeared around a drugstore, Colby broke free of the throng and raced after the suspect down an ally. When Colby reached the back of the row of shops, he came to a halt. The male in a hoodie had vanished.

Colby bent over and unhooked Duke's leash. "Find."

Duke shot forward, sniffing the air. At a large trash bin, he stopped and sat. Colby slid his gun from the holster at his waist and peered inside the dumpster. At first glance, he didn't see anything but garbage—until he glimpsed what looked like part of the navy-blue hoodie the person was wearing.

"I know you're in there. Stand up slowly with your hands up in the air. If you didn't do anything wrong, you won't be arrested. If I have to call backup to get you out of there, you'll be taken to the police headquarters."

The runner slowly stood in the midst of the smelly trash with his arms held above his head. "I ain't done nothing."

"Good. I need you to move slowly to the edge and hop down."

The young suspect stared at Duke. "He won't hurt me, will he?"

"My dog won't do anything unless I tell him to do it." Was this the bomber who ran because he saw Colby and his canine? Colby signaled to his Rottweiler to check out the man next to the dumpster.

The runner stiffened, but Duke didn't indicate any scent of a bomb on the guy.

"What's your name?" Colby asked as he patted down the young man.

"Simon Patterson."

"You can lower your arms. Do you have a photo ID to verify your identity?"

Simon reached around slowly, withdrew his wallet out of his back pocket, and flipped it open to show his driver's license.

Colby took hold of the billfold and called in to check if there were any outstanding warrants for Patterson.

"Yes, Simon Patterson has a charge of driving while his license was suspended and a failure to appear in court on that charge."

Colby disconnected the call. "Put your hands behind your back." He pulled out his handcuffs, clicked them around the man's wrists, then headed back to the command center. He and Duke were needed at the bombsite, not taking the young guy to the police station.

After transferring Patterson to another officer, Colby and Duke continued combing through the crowd. He received a call from the captain asking him to search through the area where the explosion happened at the back of the store now that the crime scene had been declared safe. They wanted to find every piece of the bomb's components that they could. He hoped they could find a fragment to trace its origin and then establish who bought it. Also, they needed to compare this bomb's fragments with the bombs left at the rug gallery and

IFI to determine if the same person was behind all three.

As Colby and Duke made their way toward the spot of the explosion, he scanned what was left of the grocery store. Two EMTs transported a person on a gurney toward their ambulance. How many were hurt or killed in this attack? What was the link between this site and the others? Was there a connection or was it all totally random? And even worse, would there be more, or would the bomber be satisfied with what happened today?

* * *

Beth hadn't heard from Colby since early this morning. Although most of the employees at IFI were home today, the news flew through the IFI building about the explosion at the grocery store, which had killed two people and injured twelve others—several in critical condition. When Beth heard about it, she'd been at her desk, and all she could think about was it could have been them. For fifteen minutes, that was all she concentrated on. She would have been on the list of dead victims since the bomb would have gone off at the time she usually fixed the coffee. Until this moment, she hadn't fully contemplated the truth. The realization hit her like a sledgehammer. A chill swept down her body.

"Beth."

She blinked and glanced to the side. "Mr. Knight, can I help you?"

He smiled. "No, but I can help you. Go home. After what you went through yesterday, you don't need to be here. You need to rest and talk to one of the counselors working with our employees who need help dealing with what happened yesterday."

"It's not just the attempted bombing here at IFI or the break-in. I feel…" She couldn't think of a good word to describe what she felt. Betrayed by Thomas. Numb at times. Anger at other times. She wanted to talk to Colby.

"Beth?"

Again, she blinked. "Sorry. I was

thinking."

He passed a card to her. "Dr. Sarah Collins is excellent at her job. She's also a member of our church. Please think about it, especially with someone breaking into your house the day before the bombing attempt here. Of course, you have more to deal with."

She casually knew who the doctor was, but she went to the early service while Sarah attended the later one. "I have work to do."

"Is the reason you don't want to leave because of the break-in?"

She shook her head. "I'm staying with Ann Maxwell until the security system is installed next Monday."

"That's great. Ann is such a dear woman. I know you don't have family here, but Ann is a perfect substitute. She's a good listener."

"Yes." And a matchmaker to boot. She sighed and pulled her purse out of her bottom drawer. "You're right. I haven't dealt with what has happened." She rose. "But I'll be back tomorrow morning at the usual time."

"Good. I'll want your opinion on the new security procedures tomorrow."

Beth left the building and made her way toward her car. Something sparkled on the ground around the driver's side of the vehicle. She blinked against the bright sun and lifted her gaze to the car window. Shards of cracked glass that had not fallen to the ground clung together in sharp points.

Stopping, she looked around the less than full parking lot. She was alone, but the feel of someone's gaze upon her wouldn't lessen.

She approached her vehicle. The glass crunched beneath her shoes. She leaned back and looked around her again. The feeling of being watched still enveloped her, though not one person entered or left the building.

Then she spied the flat back tire as well as the front one. Both slit. While hurrying around to the other side, she fumbled for her cell phone. She released a long breath. At least she only had to buy two new tires this time instead of the four Thomas had slashed previously, but she would have to replace her window. After she reported the vandalism, she used the camera on her cell phone to take pictures of the damage. The police were tied up at the moment but would contact her as soon as possible. She wasn't surprised because of the bombing, but she wanted a record of her call to 9-1-1.

As she reached for the handle, her hand shook. She made it a point not to keep anything of value in her car. It had to be Thomas. When she glanced at the driver's seat, she froze. Her legs turned to jelly, and she began to sink to the asphalt. She clutched her door to keep herself upright. Her attention never wavered from the driver's seat where a photo of her half-dressed in her bedroom lay on the black leather.

Minutes later, she wrenched her gaze from the picture captured by one of the cameras in her house. After she called a tow truck to take her to a tire store, she had to sit. She used a tissue to move the photo to the passenger front seat, with the image face down. Then she brushed the pieces of the window off the leather before she sat. When she finally climbed behind the steering wheel while waiting for the tow truck, all she could think about was how long the cameras had been in her house. Repulsion flooded her, and nausea roiled her stomach.

She had to push the feeling away or Thomas would win.

The Lord is my Rock, and I'm hanging on tightly. The whole time she kept assessing her surroundings as though Thomas was nearby and planning to assault her while she hung onto her thoughts about God. *I'm not alone. You are with me.*

She finally grabbed her cell phone and called Colby, realizing he might not be able to answer. If nothing else, she'd leave a message about what happened. The bombing would be the police department's top priority, and it should be.

"Hi. Is something wrong?" Colby asked on the fifth ring.

"I hate to interrupt you on the job, but

when I left IFI, I found my driver's side window smashed, two of my tires slashed, and a photo on the seat that had to be from the camera in my bedroom. I have a tow truck coming to take my car to Frank's Tire Shop. Then I'm going to get my window fixed. I know the police are focused on the bombing, so I took pictures of what was done to my car as well as the photo on the seat."

"Good. I'm still at the grocery store making sure we get all the bomb fragments from the site. Duke's found quite a few. I'm calling Nick to let him know what happened."

"Thanks." Beth caught sight of a tow truck coming into the parking lot. "I've got to go. My ride's here."

Thirty minutes later at the tire store, Beth settled into a chair in the waiting room, her tension still a hard knot in her stomach. She decided to go outside and call Dr. Sarah Collins for an appointment. She needed a way to deal with this stress. Maybe talking to her would help.

When her cell phone rang, she quickly

answered it, noting Nick Davidson's name on the screen.

"Colby called me about your car and the photo. Before I left the station yesterday, I found the police report on the damage done to your car seven months ago. Thomas Carson was interviewed, but there was no evidence that he did it other than he didn't have an alibi during the time your tires were sliced."

"I know, and that's why I moved and got a restraining order against him. He called me up when he found out about the restraining order and yelled at me words I won't repeat. But after that, nothing else happened. I thought the restraining order settled everything until the break-in and the cameras were found in my house. This is something Thomas would have done."

"I went by his apartment and work this morning. His SUV was gone from the parking lot at The Village, but he hasn't shown up for work or called to tell them he wasn't coming in."

"He could be in his apartment. He sometimes loaned his SUV to a friend."

"Who?"

"Brad Watson."

"I'll contact Watson, but at this time I don't have enough evidence to get a warrant to search Carson's place. I'm heading to IFI to check the parking lot cameras to see if we can ID who slashed your tires and smashed your window. If the cameras caught him, we'll have probable cause. I'll keep you informed."

"As much as I appreciate you taking the time, I don't want to take you away from the bomb investigation."

"I'm working both. A lot of federal teams are here now to help. If Carson is hassling you, he's stepped up the harassment, especially if he's been spying on you."

"Thank you."

After talking with Colby and Nick, she didn't feel as alone as she had when dealing with Thomas in the past. She took in several deep breaths and released them slowly as she punched in the phone number of Dr. Collins. When the call ended with the receptionist, Beth had an appointment in several hours. She slipped her cell into her pocket and lifted her gaze.

A white SUV was parked across the street from the tire store.

EIGHT

Beth sat in a comfortable chair across from Dr. Collins who was no more than five feet two inches with short brown hair and hazel eyes. For the first time today, Beth was calm as she discussed Thomas and the changes that she'd seen in him through their relationship and those things that she suspected he was doing to her even today. "When I looked out the window of the tire store, I saw a white SUV. I couldn't stop my hands from shaking."

"Why?"

"All I could think was that it was Thomas's car. He's harassed me for months, but I don't think it was his. The

SUV drove off within seconds after I saw it. I'm pretty sure a woman was driving. But the reaction to seeing it sparked momentary panic. I feel so vulnerable and don't know what to do. Just thinking it might be him sets me off."

"You've been proactive. The police are aware of what occurred months ago as well as recently and are looking into it. You're staying with Ann until your house has a good security system. You're talking about getting a guard dog. You're being alert and attuned to your surroundings. You aren't wringing your hands while sitting here. Maybe it's time to turn to your faith and give this to the Lord. Pray and keep doing what you're doing. Stay vigilant." Sarah gave her card to Beth then stood. "Call me if you need someone to listen to you. I'm here for you."

Beth shook hands with Sarah. "Thanks. I need to remember not to panic but to pray instead. Since the break-in, all I've been doing is panicking."

Sarah walked to her desk, wrote something on a pad, then returned to Beth, holding a piece of paper out for her to take. "I have a friend who works with canines. He may be able to find you a guard dog. Call him and tell him I sent you."

"Colby has a friend too that might be able to help. Again, thanks." Beth left Sarah's office with hope. When she looked at the past couple of days, she faced one problem after another, but there was always someone there to help her. That was the Lord working for her.

A few hours later, she returned to Ann's house with two new tires and a driver's side window. She called Ann to let her know she was in her driveway. Earlier, Ann had talked to Beth and told her to park in her garage. Colby's grandmother moved some boxes and had enough room for her Chevy. Obviously, Colby had let her know what happened in the IFI parking lot.

"Colby won't be home until later. He told me not to wait for him for dinner. He'll get something to eat before coming home. Did you have a big lunch?"

Until Ann asked her about eating, she hadn't realized she hadn't since breakfast.

"I didn't have anything."

"Then let's order a large pizza. And for dessert, I have a half-gallon of cookie dough ice cream. I'm ready to pig out."

Beth laughed. "Actually, that sounds great."

Later, when Beth finished eating more pizza and ice cream than she had in years, she collapsed in a lounge chair, groaning. "That was delicious, but I'll need to limit doing this to once a year. I'm going to have to find an exercise that I'll enjoy."

Sitting in the chair on the other side of an end table between Beth and her, Ann said, "One of the perks of being over seventy is I don't have to worry about that like you young'uns."

Beth grinned. "Thank you, Ann, for this evening. After the day I had, this time with you has been uplifting, especially the stories about Colby when he was growing up."

"I knew before he did, that he would do something to help people when he grew up, and I wasn't surprised at all that he became a canine police officer. He loved animals and was always rescuing abandoned ones."

The sound of the front door opening sent Beth to her feet. It had to be Colby, but she wanted to see for herself. Duke trotted toward the kitchen, probably for his water bowl, while Colby stood in the middle of the entry hall, his shoulders sagging forward, his head down as he stared at the tile floor. When he lifted his gaze and connected with hers, exhaustion-filled eyes stared back at her.

"Did you take the time to eat dinner?" Beth asked.

He shook his head.

"How about lunch?"

"No."

"Then I'll make you a sandwich. You need to eat something." She started for the kitchen, stopped, and looked back.

Colby stared at the floor.

"I'm a good listener. I imagine today was a difficult one. You were there for me on Monday and Tuesday. Let me be here for you now."

Ann exited the living room and crossed

the foyer, covering a yawn with her hand. "Your body needs food, Colby. Good night, y'all." She continued shuffling toward the hallway to the bedrooms. "Let Beth take care of you."

"How can you argue with such a wise grandmother?" Beth resumed her trek to the kitchen and began making a chicken salad sandwich.

Colby entered the room, opened the refrigerator, and poured iced tea into a glass. "Do you want any?"

"Yes, please." Beth took the plate with the sandwich to the table.

He set a full glass next to his food and another on the placemat catty-cornered from his.

"Do you want to talk about today?"

"No." He settled into his chair. "Yes."

Beth sipped her tea. "Were you at the site all day?"

"Yes." Colby took a bite of his dinner. "Mmm. Nana makes a great chicken salad. Is your car fixed?"

She nodded. "Nick called me after I got a new window for the car. He went to IFI to check the cameras for the parking lot. Thomas and his SUV were caught on it near your car, but the angle of the camera didn't show he vandalized your Chevy. Nick got a warrant to search Thomas's apartment. I haven't heard anything yet."

"It's probably because there's evidence from the grocery store that has to be tracked down first."

"Of course. Did you find any clues with the bomb fragments?"

"It's the same type as the others." He ate some more of his sandwich and washed it down with his drink. "While Duke and I searched the debris, we found another body. The death count is now three. It was a seven-year-old boy who wasn't feeling well, so he didn't go to school. Instead, he went to work with his father, the store's assistant manager. He was in his dad's office." He stared at his plate. The color bled from his face.

Beth clasped his lower arm. "I don't know how you do your job. I can't imagine finding a dead adult let alone a child."

"Duke discovered his foot, and I began

tossing the rubbish off the boy, hoping he was alive, but…" Colby swallowed hard. "He wasn't. Most of the time, I can remain detached while on the job. This time I couldn't."

The anguish in his voice twisted her heart. Beth clasped his shoulder. "There's nothing wrong in that. You're human. How about the cameras? Any indication of the bomber on them."

"No. There wasn't any surveillance in the stock area, but there was in the front part of the store. What footage there was is being combed through as well as what we can get from traffic cams and other places around the grocery store. Thankfully, the video was saved to the cloud."

"How about IFI's security cameras?"

"So far what we've gotten from IFI hasn't produced the guy. There are blind spots, and the bomber seemed to know them. The same with the rug gallery."

"It sounds like he stakes out the places first, trying to figure out how to get around the security cameras."

"Yeah. We need to find him before he

strikes again." Colby shoved his chair back and pushed to his feet. He started to pick up his plate.

Beth reached out and stopped him. "I'll take care of this. Go to bed."

"Duke needs to go outside."

"I'll take care of that too."

He moved closer and took her hand. "You look as tired as I feel. I'll see to Duke while you put the plate and glasses in the dishwasher."

As he went outside with Duke, Beth cleaned up the small mess she made then waited for Colby to come inside with his dog. When he did, Duke trotted ahead of them down the hallway to the bedrooms, entering Colby's ahead of him.

Colby paused and turned toward her, framing her face. "I wish I could give you answers about the break-in and where Carson is."

"Your first priority is the bomb investigation. That's how it must be, especially because of Duke. Nick will let me know when he has information."

"I know." His thumbs caressed her

upper cheeks before he dropped his hands away.

She missed his touch. She stood on her tiptoes and kissed his cheek.

"If you still want a guard dog, the friend I told you about has one. I'll try to find a time, depending on my work schedule, to take you to meet the dog on Saturday."

"Yes, I'm free to go. If that doesn't work out, Sarah Collins suggested someone today who might have a dog for me."

"Who?"

Beth had slipped the piece of paper into her pocket. She removed it. "It's Joe Wilson."

"That's my friend. Let's hope it works out."

"I'll pray it does and that the bomber is caught by then."

"'Me too." He leaned down and kissed the top of her head then stepped back. "We both need our sleep."

"Agreed." If she could sleep. She wasn't sure she could with all that was running around in her head. Two threats were out there—Thomas and some unknown bomber. If the guy followed the same pattern, he'd strike tomorrow. It started Monday, and each day, there had been one real bomb. Would it end finally because today's bomb went off, or would there be more?

* * *

Thursday afternoon, Colby met up with Nick at The Village Apartments and headed inside to Carson's place. The white SUV hadn't been in the parking lot. While the detective went upstairs to see if Carson would answer the door, Colby headed to the manager's office and showed her a copy of the warrant.

The middle-aged woman shook his hand. "I'm Aubrey Zimmer. I'll get my keys. I haven't seen him in the last couple of days. In fact, I was going to pay him a visit. He's late on the rent."

"Is he late often?"

"Actually, this is the first time. He might be late on his payment because his brother's here visiting, and they haven't been around a lot."

Colby, with Duke by his side, took the stairs to the second floor with Ms. Zimmer.

Nick stood waiting. "I'm Detective Nick Davidson," he said to the manager. "I've rung the bell several times, but no one's answered."

Ms. Zimmer pulled out her set of keys, found the one she needed, and unlocked Carson's apartment.

"Please return to your place," Colby said to the manager as Nick stepped inside, quickly followed by Colby and Duke.

Nick closed the front door. "I just got the fingerprint report on the cameras you recovered from Beth Sherman's house. There was one with a readable thumbprint. There were a few others on the evidence, but they were smudged except for one clear partial. The thumbprint was matched with Carson from his military record. He received a general discharge from the army for questionable conduct toward a female soldier. I put a BOLO out on Carson. Now we need to find more evidence to tie him to the break-in at Beth's house and for harassing her."

"Thanks for being on top of this." Colby wished he'd been able to follow through on Beth's case, but at least something had been done in the midst of a bomber practically holding the city hostage.

First, they determined no one was in the apartment before they began looking for evidence that Carson was involved in putting cameras in Beth's house. They also wanted to prove he'd been harassing her after the restraining order had been issued. Every time Colby thought of what the man had done to Beth, his anger escalated.

Colby stepped into the single bedroom and let Duke off his leash. Out of habit, Colby gave his canine the command to search. For all he knew, Carson could be involved in the bombings, especially with the sighting of a white SUV on the traffic cam near the grocery store early Wednesday morning, but the license plate number was muddied over. And also for each day a bomb had been planted, the man had been hard to find.

While his dog sniffed the air, Colby

scanned the area to see if anything stood out to him before he combed through the closet and drawers. The wooden desk with a printer on it and drawers on both sides drew his attention. Its top was covered in dust except for a spot the size of a computer.

Questions streamed through his mind. What was on the computer? Pictures like the one left on the front seat in Beth's car? Had Thomas left with the laptop? Why take it with him? Was he coming back?

A familiar sound intruded into his thoughts. Out of the corner of his eye, Colby glimpsed Duke sitting in front of the closet door, scratching to get inside.

"Find something, Duke?

He turned the knob to let his dog into a big walk-in closet, full of clothes and other items. Duke padded toward the back and sat in front of an empty space under shirts hanging above. As he did when he found something to do with a bomb, his dog stared at the place. The rest of the area was jammed with boxes, shoes, and duffel bags underneath the clothing. Duke wasn't interested in any of that—only in the empty space.

"Good job, Duke." Colby gave him his favorite squeaky toy.

He didn't have a good feeling about this. What else could Duke find in the living room and kitchen? Whatever his dog smelled, it had to do with a bomb. Was Carson the bomber? Who was the person visiting him?

"Colby, come in here," Nick said. "I found something."

NINE

Colby returned to the living room in Carson's apartment. "Duke homed in on a place in the closet that had a scent of a bombing ingredient, but there isn't anything there."

Nick frowned. "Interesting. Duke can tell a bomb ingredient when it's not there?"

"Yes, it's possible. The carpet where the ingredient had been would retain the scent. That's why Duke and I move through a crowd at a bombing site. A person handling a bomb will often retain a scent for Duke to focus in on."

"Then Carson could be a suspect in the bombing yesterday."

Colby nodded. "What did you find?"

Nick held up a stack of photos. He passed them to Colby.

As he flipped through the pictures of Beth in her house, his anger grew until all he wanted to do was to rip up each photo and throw the trash away. He couldn't wait until he caught Carson and made sure he paid for his actions. Now, more than ever, he needed to go through the man's computer and see what he'd done to Beth beyond what Colby knew. How long had Carson been watching her? Were these all the photos? What did he intend to do with the pictures? But Colby had one overriding question. Did Carson make the bombs?

Lord, I know I haven't come to You much in years, but please help me minimize the damage to Beth's reputation if Carson put her pictures up online, and above all, help me find the bomber.

"Colby, are you okay?" his high school friend asked, worry in his voice.

"I will be when we find Carson. Even though I never met the guy until recently, from what Beth told me, I knew he was bad news." Colby was glad he'd been at his grandmother's on Monday. "We need forensics to come here and test the carpet in the bedroom closet. In the meantime, I'll have Duke go through the rest of the apartment."

* * *

Beth pulled into the garage at Ann's house after a full day at IFI. Appointments had been set up for the employees to talk to counselors throughout the week at the very least. Dr. Sarah Collins was one who'd been there this afternoon, and Beth met with her again. Yesterday, Sarah had helped her, and today she gave her some more suggestions on how to deal with the stress and fear.

Beth hoped she could get a guard dog soon. She needed to exercise, and although she wasn't into jogging, she would like to walk at the park or in her neighborhood but couldn't do it alone with Thomas in hiding, according to what Colby had mentioned earlier. A guard dog would give her the freedom to exercise, and she would enjoy it and feel safe at the same time.

Ann opened the garage door into the house. "How was your day?"

"Better. I met with Sarah again. It helps to talk." Beth entered the kitchen. "Colby called me to let me know that Thomas Carson has disappeared. The police have a BOLO out on him. He may not even be in town anymore." The thought lifted her spirits and eased her fears. Sarah was right. *Keep your eye on the Lord and turn the fear over to Him*.

"Good. But something needs to be done to that man for harassing you." Ann shook her head as she made her way to the teapot. After pouring the hot liquid into two mugs, she brought it to the table and gestured toward Beth. "Sit. He'll be brought to justice."

"First, they have to find him. I dated Thomas and can't believe I didn't see what type of person he truly is. The man I saw when I first started dating him was so different from the man he was at the end. What drives someone to put cameras in my house to spy on me? It's hard to understand."

"I don't know for sure. I could guess anger, possibly fear."

"I didn't see that when we first met. That makes me question my ability really to see a person for who he is." Beth thought back to the past few days and her developing feelings for Colby. He'd been there when she needed him. He had supported her. He had made her feel safe in the midst of all that was going on.

"I won't deny that some people can camouflage who they are for a while, but in the end, it'll come out. It's hard to stifle your true personality for a long time." Ann sipped her tea.

The sound of the front door opening and closing caused Beth to stiffen until Duke trotted into the kitchen. Colby followed behind him, and she relaxed back against her chair. "How did it go at Thomas's apartment?" He'd told her a BOLO had been put out for Thomas, but he didn't have time to tell her much more.

"I have a few calls I need to make."

Ann stood and scurried from the room.

Colby opened the back door to let Duke outside then took the chair Ann had vacated. "How did it go at work today?"

"Better than yesterday."

"What do you think of the extra security methods they're putting into place?"

"That's exactly what Mr. Knight asked me today. I told him it was sad that it's come to locking up a building so tight that it takes at least five or ten minutes to get inside."

Colby nodded. "I agree, but it's necessary, especially so the employees and bystanders are aware of their surroundings."

"Any leads where Thomas might be?"

"I wish. A couple of leads didn't pan out. According to Ms. Zimmer, Carson has had a visitor for the past few days—his brother. I couldn't find any information on any brother or much about Carson's past."

"Thomas never talked about any siblings. In fact, I thought he was an only child."

"So, it's possible the other guy at his

apartment isn't related."

"Do you have a picture of this guy?"

"Sorta. The only cameras in the apartment building are at the entrances and every time the guy we think is Carson's brother enters, he has his head down or turned away from the camera. We can ascertain an approximate height and he has a medium build." Colby's cell phone rang, and he quickly answered it.

While he was speaking with Nick, Beth made her way to the counter and poured more tea into her mug. In the short time she'd known Colby, she realized she knew more about his past than she ever did about Thomas's.

She returned to her chair as Colby disconnected his call. "Any good news?"

"I'm not sure if it's good or bad, but Carson's social security number isn't really his. It's one for a man who died seven years ago. Nick is checking the information about the deceased man, who was forty years old. His name was Tom Carson. It looks like he bought a new identity."

Chill bumps rose on her arms. She

folded them across her chest. "Then who was Thomas if that wasn't even his real name? Why did he change his identity?"

"Good questions. I'm circulating his photo to see who he might really be."

And she never had an indication that Thomas wasn't who he said he was.

He cupped her hand lying on the table between them. "Hopefully, all this will help you." He paused and stared at their physical connection for a few seconds before looking up into her eyes. "There's something else that I've been struggling to find a way to tell you."

"What? You can tell me anything. You've done so much to help me."

Colby sucked in a deep breath and released it slowly. "Nick found a stack of photos of you that had to be taken from the cameras in your house. He's running the fingerprints himself. He'll keep them private, but if this goes to trial, it might become a different matter."

Beth curled her hand into a fist beneath his. "I want the harassment to quit, but I don't want to go to trial over the photos."

Her throat jammed with anger. She swallowed several times before she could ask, "Do you think those were all he had?"

"I don't know. We're looking into it. If we find his computer, we might know more."

There was a part of her that had feared there would be something like physical photos or ones appearing online. But the other part had prayed there wouldn't be. She'd done nothing wrong. She had to remember that fact if others found out about the pictures. "When I knew him, he had a laptop. He kept it on his desk in his bedroom when he wasn't using it. Several times, he asked me to get it for him. He loved to cook but sometimes forgot an ingredient of a recipe he had stored on his computer. I have to admit I'm not a good cook. The basics is all I do. I think I inherited that from my mom. She didn't like to cook. Dad usually brought food home for dinner." Her nervous prattling showcased her agitation. The idea of others seeing her…She couldn't finish that thought.

"I bet you could talk Nana into showing you how. She's great and has spoiled me in the short time I've been here."

"Me too."

He clasped her hand between both of his. "You aren't alone. The bomber will be caught and so will Thomas. Then you'll be safe."

"You make me feel safe," Beth said before thinking what that implied. She cared for Colby more than she thought she could after Thomas's bad treatment. He was still out there planning other ways to get back at her because she broke it off. His invasion of privacy left her shaken, and she couldn't seem to get beyond that. Sarah told her to turn her fear over to the Lord. Beth was also having a hard time letting the anger go with all that was happening in Cimarron City.

"I have some good news. I should be able to take you to get a guard dog this Saturday afternoon."

"Great! If he's even half of what Duke is, he'll be wonderful."

His warm look gave her flutters in her

stomach.

"Let's hope tomorrow is quiet like today. We have some leads to follow."

"Amen."

* * *

After checking in on Friday at the police station, Colby received a text message to come see Nick. Colby and Duke stopped by the detective's office. He hoped there was good news about the bombing and Carson's illegal activities. "Any new evidence or clues?"

"Yes, I just got the report on Carson's apartment. The most important thing was that the bomb's main ingredient, C-4 plastic explosives, was confirmed present at the apartment where Duke smelled it in the closet as well as on the kitchen table, which probably was where the bombs were put together."

"So, Carson is the bomber. Now it's only a matter of finding the man. Today I intend to check The Village when I can in case Carson shows up there. But now,

Duke and I will go by the construction company and check on their inventory of work-site explosives. If Carson is the bomber as we think, most likely, that's where he got some of the ingredients for his bombs."

Nick rose from behind his desk. "I agree, and I'm coming with you."

"Good. Carson is a threat to Beth, and I hope to be involved in bringing him in."

"His photo will be released to the public as a person of interest in the bombing. It will no doubt be picked up nationally too." Nick showed Colby the picture that would be used. "Maybe someone will call in a sighting of Carson or who he really is."

"Let's hope we can find him before another bomb is left somewhere."

Colby and Duke headed into the hallway with Nick. "Any evidence of the identity of the visitor at Carson's apartment? I think he's involved because there were two people in the break-in of Beth's house on Monday—the man who left her place and the person picking him up and driving the SUV. There were some other fingerprints found in Carson's apartment. Any matches? He could be part of the bombing too."

"Besides Carson's, there were good prints of two unknown people and the rest were smudges. Those two people don't have their fingerprints on file. There's no decent video footage of this guy visiting Carson. He's very good at evading a security camera."

"If we find Carson's computer, it has the video footage of Beth's house on it, and if this guy was the one coming out of her house rather than Carson, we may get a good picture of him that way." Colby's gut tightened with rage when he thought about Carson and his friend spying on Beth in her home.

As Nick left the police station, he walked besides Colby. "I hope we can get a good photo of the second guy. In the meantime, I'll be asking tenants at The Village if they can describe what this mysterious guy looks like. How long has he been here? Do any of them know where he is?"

"I'll meet you at the construction

company." Colby parted from Nick in the parking lot behind headquarters.

On the drive to where Carson worked, Colby called Beth to let her know that Carson's photo would be on the news. "How's it going today?"

"Good. Getting work done after several days of chaos. How's your day going?"

"I'm going to Turner Construction."

"You've found Thomas. He's at work?" Hope filled her voice.

"Carson's picture will be shown all over the place as a person of interest in the bombing case."

"Thomas? He's the bomber?"

"Possibly." He couldn't tell her the details yet. "With his photo everywhere, hopefully, he'll be found soon, and then you can get answers about his harassment. That could be the least of his problems."

"Thanks for letting me know. Are we still on to go look at your friend's guard dog tomorrow?"

"Yes, but that could always change. Joe won't sell him to anyone else before giving you a chance to see the German shepherd." Colby pulled into the parking lot near the main building at the construction company. "I'll see you later today. Gotta go."

"Bye. Take care of yourself."

Colby turned his speakerphone off, exited his car, and put Duke's leash on him. Nick parked next to him and joined Colby as they walked toward the main office.

He held Duke on a short lead. "While we drove here, I called John Turner, the owner. He'll meet us—"

A tall, muscular man about fifty walked out of the building and greeted them with a firm handshake. "Beautiful dog you have," Turner said to Colby.

"He's a bomb-sniffing canine. I'd like to have him check your warehouse and any other buildings. Thomas Carson is a person of interest in the bombing case, and he had access to your explosives for your construction sites."

Turner frowned. "And that's why I'm here. If that's the case, I need to put additional policies in place to make sure no one steals the ingredients to cause an explosion or materials, like blasting caps, to build a bomb. They're always locked up in a small storeroom in our warehouse."

"Who has a key to the lock?" Nick asked as they entered the large warehouse.

"The warehouse supervisor and his assistant, me, and our demolition expert. That's it. Thomas Carson is—was the assistant in the warehouse to the supervisor."

"Does he know he isn't an assistant anymore?" Colby remembered the supervisor hadn't been too happy with Carson being "sick" or was it something else?

"He doesn't know he's been fired yet because he isn't answering our calls. According to my supervisor, Alex, Thomas Carson has been absent too many days. He'd been slacking on the job. I need someone who shows up to work and doesn't have the police coming to visit him here." Turner waved to two men across the large building. "The taller one is Alex, and the other guy is the demolition expert,

Andy."

As the men crossed the warehouse, Colby assessed the man who handled bombs as part of his job. Slender and about five feet, eight inches, Alex appeared meek, a quiet type, the opposite of the owner.

"The police are here to check our inventory of explosive materials. I need you two to show them where we keep it." The owner swung to Nick. "I have an important business call. I'll return when I'm finished." Then to Colby, Turner added, "I appreciate your dog checking my buildings, especially with all that's going on in Cimarron City."

Alex escorted them to the back of the warehouse, took out his key, and inserted it into the lock. The door to the storeroom as well as the frame around the entrance and the deadbolt all appeared sturdy. Duke exhibited his excitement by his restless behavior and eagerness to get inside.

"Who has the inventory list?" Nick asked.

"I keep one on me as well as one on the

clipboard just inside the room. Also Mr. Turner and Alex have one on their computers." The demolition expert gestured toward the list hanging on the wall to the right, opened his electronic tablet, and skimmed both records. "They're in sync."

Colby scanned the area. "Does Carson have a list of what's in this storeroom?"

"Yes, on his electronic tablet," the warehouse supervisor answered before he left them to go into the room.

"Now let's see if the list matches what you have in here." Colby took one record of the explosive inventory and gave the other to Nick. "Let's each check to make sure we haven't missed something."

"If you have questions, I'll wait here." The demolition expert closed the door and leaned back against it.

Colby started his accounting of the inventory. When he came to the C-4, the packages didn't match the number on the list. There were five missing. He listed it then continued his search. When he reached the blasting caps, more than five were missing. At the entrance, he compared his findings with Nick's.

"We both came up with five packages of C-4 missing and double the amount of blasting caps." Colby glanced at the demolition expert. "How often do you check your physical inventory against what should be here?"

"Once a week."

"When did you do that the last time?" Nick asked.

"Every Friday at the end of the day. Nothing was missing a week ago."

There were enough supplies, not used yet, to make two more bombs—that they knew of so far. More explosives could be missing from other places. Colby ground his teeth. "I suggest strongly you check at the end of every day from now on, and I'll put that in my report."

While Nick continued the conversation with the demolition expert, Colby took Duke through the warehouse to check for any scent of an explosive. There was nothing there as well as the rest of the construction site. He and Nick reported what they found to the owner.

When they left the main building, Nick paused by Colby's car. "Carson's last day at the construction company was half a day on Monday. After that, he went home sick."

"And the first bomb was placed Monday afternoon." Colby opened the back door to his police SUV, and Duke went into his crate in the cargo area that was secured in case of a wreck.

"I'm going back to headquarters to give the police chief the news about what was discovered here and push the search for Thomas Carson."

"Good. Duke and I are going to some places to check for a bomb. The first stop is an elementary school not far from here. Duke will love it. Wherever he goes, he attracts attention, especially from children."

After Nick left, Colby slipped behind the steering wheel and let headquarters know that he was going to Sooner Elementary School. As he pulled out of the parking lot, he couldn't get out of his mind that there were still enough explosive materials for two good size bombs. If Thomas Carson was the bomber, then that might explain why the floor Beth worked on at IFI was targeted. But why Prescott Rug Galley and the grocery store?

TEN

When Beth entered the kitchen, bright sunshine flooded the room. It lifted her up. The scent of bread baking and bacon frying saturated the air. She heard footsteps behind her and swung around. The sight of Colby made her spirits soar. She smiled. Today, she wanted to put the horrific week she and the people of Cimarron City had gone through behind her, and she would try her best to focus on getting a guard dog and enjoying time with Colby.

"Are we still on to go look at your friend's dog?"

"Yes. But I'm on call."

"I understand."

"You two need to eat breakfast and go look at the dog." Ann took the biscuits out of the oven, placed them on the top of the stove, then gestured toward the food. "It's ready."

Colby came to Beth's side. "This smell is what drew me."

She laughed. "Ann, this is my favorite meal of the day, especially when you cook it."

Ann beamed. "I love doing it. Having you both here has been great."

Colby swept his arm toward the oven. "Ladies first."

As they settled at the table with their plates full of food, Ann bowed her head. "Lord, bring the bomber to justice. Please protect the people of Cimarron City. Bless this food. Amen."

As Beth sipped her tea, she looked out the nook's bay window. "How far away is your friend's ranch?"

"Joe lives ten miles out of town." Colby slathered butter all over his warm biscuit then took a bite.

"Good. It won't take us long. Are you coming with us, Ann?"

She shook her head. "I have pies to make for the luncheon after the church service tomorrow."

"Do you need help?" Beth took a bite of her scrambled eggs.

"No, I want you to bring your dog home today."

"That will be up to Joe." Colby finished his last piece of bacon.

For the next few minutes, Beth ate her breakfast, eager to leave for the ranch. When she finished, she took her dishes to the sink and rinsed them off before putting them into the dishwasher.

Ann approached her with the rest of the plates and utensils. "Go. I hope this dog works out for you."

Beth chuckled. "I like helping you."

"I know. And I like helping you. Let me right now. You two don't need to rush back here. I'm going to be busy with baking the pies. And you know how I feel about cooking."

Beth hugged Ann. "You're such a special

friend. Thank you for taking me in." As she left the kitchen, her emotions clogged her throat. Being around Ann made her want to have her parents nearby. She needed to talk to her mother. She didn't want her parents, who worried all the time, to know what was happening, but she needed to hear from them. They usually moved every couple of years. Maybe she could talk to them about living in Cimarron City.

Deep in thought, she nearly ran into Colby coming around the corner. His hand shot out and steadied her. "Is everything all right, Beth?"

She grinned. "I was just thinking about my parents. I want to talk to them, but they would know something's wrong with me. I can never fool my mother if I'm upset."

"Once we find Carson, I think the city and you will be much better off and a lot calmer. Are you ready to see the dog?"

"Yeah. I need to get my purse and cell phone." She headed to the bedroom she was using, grabbed her handbag, then hurried out to Colby's truck.

"I had a Bichon Frise when I was a child. I loved her. It was so hard on me when she died that I decided not to have another pet because I didn't want to go through that again." Beth settled inside and strapped her seatbelt across her.

Colby started the engine and backed out of the driveway. "I had several pets while growing up. A couple at the same time. When I lost one, I had another to fill that void. It helped me get over the death of a pet faster."

"I moved around a lot as a child and learned not to get too settled in. It was hard saying good-bye to friends. Looking back, I think that was probably part of the reason I didn't get another dog. When I moved here, I intended to stay for a long time. Cimarron City has a small-town feel to it with some of the benefits of a city too."

"I like that about Cimarron City too." Colby turned down a gravel road to a one-story, red brick house and stopped in front of it. "Nick called me early this morning. He discovered that Carson's real identity is

Liam Quinn from Dallas. He's delving into Quinn's life."

She'd known Thomas Carson wasn't his real name but upon hearing what his real one was left her pulse rate accelerating. Had she dated a guy who might have killed people? The question chilled her. "Why would he change his name? What's he hiding? Setting off bombs before he came here?"

"All good questions I hope we can get answers to." Colby glanced toward the ranch house. "Focus on getting acquainted with your dog."

She drew in a deep breath and released it slowly. "Good advice."

When a huge man, probably ten or fifteen years older than Colby, came outside with a mostly brown, large German shepherd, Beth thought of her petite size of five feet two inches. "My Bichon was so much smaller than that one. Can I handle a dog that big?"

"Yes. He's been well trained by Joe. You'll be fine. I'll help you."

"When I was child, a neighbor had a big

dog that used to always bark and snarl when I went past his fence. He was a mixed breed and in my six-year-old mind, enormous in size. Part of him was German shepherd. I didn't think about that incident until I saw Joe's dog."

"You're used to Duke."

"Yes, because you've trained him well."

"Then you'll be fine. As a teenager, Joe was a role model. He taught me a lot about dogs and working with them. He's part of the reason I wanted to be a canine police officer."

She opened her door. "When you said he was a friend when you lived here before, I thought you all were the same age."

"He was one of my coaches. He showed me how to train dogs. He was first a mentor then a friend." Colby climbed from his car at the same time as Beth.

Joe stepped off the porch, leaving the German shepherd behind, and greeted Beth first.

"I appreciate you seeing me today." She shook Joe's hand while Colby rounded the car and joined them. "Is this the guard dog?"

"Yes. His name's Gabe." Joe clapped Colby on his back. "Good to see you're back in Cimarron City. It's about time you came home."

Colby laughed. "I didn't have a reason until now."

"Are you ready to move on?"

"I wish I had time to talk, but I'm on call. I'll make sure you and I spend time together when this bomber is stopped."

"If anyone can find the bomber, it's you." Joe turned toward Beth and waved his hand toward the dog. "This is Gabe. He'll be one year old at the end of the month."

The German shepherd sat in front of Beth.

"Can I pet him?"

Joe grinned. "Of course."

Beth bent over and ran her hand from the top of Gabe's head to partway down his back. "He's beautiful. Where does he like to be rubbed the most?"

"Behind his ears."

Beth's earlier tension siphoned from her

body. "I know with training you give out rewards when a dog does what you're teaching him. What kind of reward does he like?"

"Two things. A doggie treat called Yummy and a squeaky rubber duck toy. I'll give you a bag of Yummy treats and the toy." Joe pointed to the side of the house. "Let's go out back and I'll show you what Gabe can do. I'd like you to work with him today and several times next week. The more you bond with Gabe the better it will be."

"Like Duke and Colby? They work as a team."

"Not quite the same. They're a team searching for something. In Duke's case, bomb ingredients. But the team bonding with Gabe is the same. When you're a team, he'll sense when you're stressed or in trouble. He's there to assure you that you're safe."

As they walked around to the back, Colby sat in a lounge chair on the patio, watching her.

She glanced back at him and smiled.

The minute she began petting Gabe she realized she should have gotten a dog a long time ago.

Joe stood yards away with Gabe next to him. "Call him to come to you."

"What do I say?"

"Come, Gabe. You can signal him by doing this." Palm upward, Joe curled his fingers into a loose fist.

Beth spent the next half hour getting to know Gabe and practicing the voice and hand signals the German shepherd responded to. By the time she left with Colby, she felt optimistic. A dog like Gabe would be a deterrent to Thomas, who hated dogs. The more she worked with Gabe, the more comfortable she was, pushing away her reservation about how large Gabe was.

"You two fit together," Colby said as he started his truck. "After my shift on Tuesday, I'll bring you back here to work with Gabe and Joe again before you take him home that day. If you want to stay at Nana's house longer, that's fine. She told me to tell you that. Duke and Gabe would get along."

Tuesday evening would be the first night she'd be back in her home after the break-in. The security system would be in, and she would have Gabe. She'd be able to do it. She couldn't keep staying with Ann. "I appreciate everything you and Ann have done for me. But I have to go back, and I might as well on Tuesday. In fact, on Wednesday night, I'd like to invite you and Ann to come to dinner at my house. It's my turn to pay you two back for your help."

"You don't have to."

"I know, but I want to. When I came here, this town was to be my home for years. I don't want Thomas to change that. When he harassed me, I thought about finding another job and leaving Cimarron City, but I didn't want to leave if possible. So, I moved to my house. It was across town. I'd hoped Thomas would stop when he didn't see me at the apartment complex. I thought he had when nothing happened to me for six months."

Colby pulled into his grandmother's driveway and turned off the engine. He twisted toward her. "When he's found, he'll be arrested. We have enough evidence to bring him in for at least breaking into your home and installing cameras. And that doesn't even address his possible link to the bombings."

"I've been saving up for a vacation. Instead, I'm using that money to get a security system and a guard dog, but strangely, after today, it doesn't bother me. When I petted Gabe, I realized how much I missed having a dog."

"I can't imagine being without one." Colby exited his vehicle at the same time as Beth and waited while she rounded the hood.

She stopped inches away. Her gaze connected with his. Although meeting him only five days ago, she felt as if she knew him better than she'd known Thomas, and she'd spent months with him. At night when she tried to fall asleep, she would think about Colby. He made her smile even when she didn't feel like doing it. She trusted him.

"This will be over soon. With all the law enforcement officers in the state looking for

Carson, we'll find him." Closing the space between them, he cupped her face and leaned forward, his mouth a whisper away from hers. "I'm not going to let him hurt you." His lips brushed over hers.

The ring of Colby's phone disrupted the moment. He pulled back and dug into his pant pocket to retrieve his cell. "Parker here." The relaxed expression on his face instantly vanished as frown lines appeared. "I'll be right there."

When he disconnected his phone, Beth asked, "What happened?"

"There's been another bombing."

ELEVEN

Colby hurried toward his grandmother's house to get Duke, his gun, and his badge. "The bombing isn't at a business," he said to Beth who was keeping up with him. "It's near the lake. Not sure what blew up. Possibly a cabin. It was just reported. I'll let you know when I can."

While Colby gathered what he needed, Beth stood by the door, the color draining from her face. Nana joined her.

He called Duke at the same time he went into his bedroom and buckled on his gun belt. He pinned on his badge and left. At the front door, he glanced from Beth to his grandmother. "I'll be all right. Stay here. Don't go anywhere."

Striding toward his truck with Duke, he realized he'd probably scared Beth and Nana, but frankly, he wanted them to stay where they were until he knew what was going down. Why set off a bomb at the lake outside of town? The marina wasn't in that area. So, was it a cabin or something else?

Twenty minutes later, he climbed from his vehicle, put the leash on Duke, and headed toward the bomb sight. The fire caused by the explosion had been put out. As the dark black smoke dissipated, he saw the structure of a bombed SUV, the doors had blown off and were on the ground yards away. The rear of the vehicle was in better condition. Colby moved forward and glimpsed the license plate still on the bumper. Carson's SUV.

The firefighters continued dousing the vehicle to cool what was left. Colby and Duke couldn't do much until then. He walked to his police captain to see what he wanted him to do. "When was this reported?"

"Right before I called you. We got a

phone call from a couple who have a cabin not far from here. The explosion rocked their place. They immediately went outside. That's when they saw the SUV on fire. A firefighter told me he thinks a person was inside in the rear cargo area."

"Thomas Carson?"

"We don't know. But why would he be in the back?" his captain asked.

"Making a device that blew up. It wouldn't be the first time a bombmaker blows himself up." Would this be the last of the bombs in Cimarron City? Colby prayed it was. In the past six days, the town had been held hostage. There hadn't been a common thread among the sites that the investigators had discovered. What would the randomization of the targets mean? It could be anything from anger, a mental illness, or some connection that hadn't been found yet.

His captain frowned. "But what about the guy who visited Carson? Any news on who it was?"

"Detective Davidson discovered Thomas Carson's true identity. It's Liam Quinn.

Nick's delving into his past. The team is checking into Quinn/Carson's friends and family as well as any person who has links to him. We do know he doesn't have a brother as the apartment manager had thought. We're looking at people connected with the rug gallery, the grocery store, and IFI. With the employees at IFI, there's a long list and a lot of relationships between two of the three."

"Yeah, a lot of them used the grocery store. My wife shopped there. The first place wasn't as frequented as The Market. We have no idea why the bomber's doing it. That's frustrating."

"If the bomber perpetrated the crimes by himself, and he's in the cargo area of the SUV, we may never know why. I've had that happen to a couple of my cases in Florida, and when I think about them today, I get frustrated." Colby noticed a firefighter signaling it was okay for him and Duke to approach.

The stench of the burnt vehicle and flesh assaulted his nostrils—and not for the first time. From the rear of the SUV, he stared at the charred remains, a person's body blown apart and in pieces. As Colby walked around the SUV, he spied a gold signet ring on the victim's scorched hand in the front seat area. Did Carson wear one? Colby didn't remember him wearing a ring when he'd confronted him. From the condition of the body, it would take a while to make an identification.

He hoped this was the end of the bombings. If Carson was preparing a new bomb and ended up blowing himself up, then this should be over, but what if another person had caused the explosion to put suspicion solely on Carson? In that case, if the person walked away, there might be a vapor trail. One of Duke's abilities as a vapor-wake dog was following the scent of a bomb ingredient in the air, especially since the wind was calm right now and the explosion only happened a half hour ago. Not the best condition for Duke, but it was worth trying.

He stepped away from the vehicle and gave Duke a long leash as he circled the SUV for any sign of an explosive trail his dog could follow. Duke suddenly veered away from the crime scene and tugged on his leash as he increased his gait toward the cabin sitting a hundred yards away.

As Colby neared what appeared to be an abandoned place, he called out, "I need back up."

Two officers jogged toward him and Duke while his dog sat at the main door. "I need to check the exterior first. Don't go in yet. The door could be rigged."

Colby circled the structure with Duke to see if he could look inside. The front door was the only entrance, and each window was covered. He couldn't tell if the place was wired with explosives. "There was only one way inside. I have to get a bomb squad robot to go in and give us a view of the interior before we enter."

While Colby waited, he went over the case. He wanted to find a reason behind the bombings, but if Carson was gone, they might never know.

* * *

Beth paced the length of Ann's living room for the next thirty minutes. Colby called earlier and said he would be returning to his grandma's house soon. Not soon enough for her.

The sound of the front door opening filled the air. She hurried into the entry hall and watched an exhausted-looking Colby coming into the house. Even Duke looked tired as he padded toward the kitchen.

"I need to feed him and make sure his water's fresh."

"It is. I changed it after eating tonight. Did you have anything for dinner?" Beth followed Colby into the kitchen.

"Yeah. I grabbed a hamburger and fries on the way home." He poured Duke's food into his bowl.

"Do you want something to drink?" Beth took the pitcher of cold tea and poured a glass full of the liquid.

Colby shook his head and took a seat at the kitchen table. "After Duke eats and goes outside, I'm ready for bed. It's been a long day.

"What happened?"

"Thomas Carson's SUV was blown up and a person in the back area died. No one was in the driver's seat. Bits and pieces of the bomb were found around the dead body parts."

"Was it Thomas?" Beth sat in a chair next to Colby.

"Don't know for sure. Does he wear a gold signet ring on his right hand?"

"Yes, he did. According to him, it was his dad's ring."

"I'll let them know at headquarters. Now that we know his real name and his alias, they'll look at his dental records as well as the hospital to see if he had any broken bones both here and in Dallas. That may take time." When Duke finished gobbling down his food, Colby stood and walked to the back door to let his dog out then returned to the table. "There was a cabin nearby that held materials for various kinds of bombs, but also a laptop. From what I heard from headquarters, it's Thomas's computer. Nick is working on the laptop and will protect your privacy concerning the photos."

Beth released a long breath. "So, it's over hopefully with the bombings and the pictures."

"We're getting closer to the truth. If the body in the SUV is Carson's, we'll be near the end. The only thing we need to wrap up is who was staying with Carson. We need to verify that he was a friend, a member of his family, or a partner in the bombing. We'll go back to The Village and interview some of the tenants as well as the apartment manager. We've determined the other person of interest appeared on Monday, the first day of the attempted bombing. But so far, no one's been able to describe him other than body type and height."

"Thomas was many things, but I still can't believe he would try to blow up people." She frowned, remembering how he'd treated her when she ended it with him. Could she really read a person correctly? Up until Thomas, she thought she could. He'd been charming and accommodating for the first several months. Then everything started falling apart. He wanted her to spend more time with him and know where she was at all times. He began complaining about her being at church half of Sunday and sometimes during the week. How could she have foreseen that? It was as though he wore a mask for the first three months then slowly removed it until she didn't recognize Thomas.

Colby went to the back door and let Duke in. "This has been an exhausting week. I may have to take a raincheck on going to church tomorrow. I'd probably fall asleep during the sermon."

"I know what you mean. It's been intense, but I have to go. We often have fifteen to twenty kids under two in the nursery. There are three of us who take care of them." Beth started for the hallway to the bedrooms. "You've gotten quite a bit of overtime in your first week."

He chuckled. "That's the bright side of what's going on. I needed that. When I decided to team up with a bomb-sniffing dog, I knew there would be times like this, but I would have rather had time to get acquainted with the police department first. Over the past twelve years, Cimarron City has changed, so I'm having to refamiliarize myself to the town I grew up in." He stopped at her bedroom, turned toward her, and cupped her face. "I look forward to things slowing down."

Her gaze linked with his. Drawn to his soft gray eyes containing a gleam, she remained still, not wanting to move away from him. He leaned forward, dipping his head toward her. She wanted him to kiss her.

When his lips settled against hers, the touch sent a streak of pleasure down her length. His hands slipped from her face, and he embraced her, drawing her against him. Seconds later, he lifted his head, released her, and stepped back. She looked up at him, a war of emotions from attraction to regret flitting across his expression.

"I'm sorry. I shouldn't have done that with all that's going on." He opened her door. "Good night. See you tomorrow."

She entered her bedroom, disappointed

and yet also agreeing with Colby. How could she make a rational decision after the chaos of the past week?

* * *

At breakfast on Sunday, Beth sat at the kitchen table eating a stack of pancakes. "These are delicious, Ann. I haven't had blueberry ones since I was a teenager. My mother and I used to go out for pancakes for breakfast once a week. It was our 'girl' time."

"I hope I can meet her when your parents come to visit you."

"I don't know if they will. I always go home to see them. They hate traveling." And yet, they moved from one place to another every two years. Maybe that was the reason they felt that way.

"That's a shame."

Beth glanced at the wall clock, stood, and brought her dishes to the sink. "I've got to leave." She rinsed her plate and utensils then put them into the dishwasher.

"I'm coming with you. Colby hasn't

gotten much sleep this week. I'll leave a note for him to come when he gets up and let him know I rode with you."

"He was exhausted last night. He might not get up until this afternoon."

"Then he needs the rest. I'll get him to church next week." Ann finished cleaning up. "I'll write the note and get my purse."

While Beth waited, she let Duke out back and filled up his bowl with fresh water. As Ann returned to the kitchen, Beth let the dog inside then she and Ann headed into the garage. Ten minutes later, Beth parked her car in the church lot. While Ann was helping to prepare for the lunch after the last service, Beth went to the first church service then her adult Sunday class before she worked in the nursery while some parishioners went to the late service.

Beth kept looking to see if Colby showed up, but by the time she needed to go to the nursery, he hadn't appeared. She wasn't really surprised. It had been hard for her to roll out of bed and get ready for church. But now, thanks to three cups of coffee, she was wide awake.

Beth entered the nursery, excited to put the past week out of mind while she enjoyed holding and playing with the children. For the next twenty minutes, there were eighteen girls and boys under two who were dropped off. Beth stood at the half door taking diaper bags and kids while the parents signed them in.

When the rush at the nursery entrance calmed and the late service started, Beth twisted around and scanned the large room. Nearby, Kathy, a six-month-old baby, started crying. Beth scooped her up into her arms, checked her diaper and realized Kathy needed it changed. Beth grabbed the baby's bag and took Kathy into a small side room to change her diaper. After she took care of the problem, she picked up the baby, cuddling the child against her.

Beth walked toward the tall trashcan in the corner, stepped on the pedal, and dropped the diaper into it. Her attention fell on the opened door into the room. Behind it lay a backpack exactly like the one she'd discovered at IFI.

TWELVE

Beth hurried into the main room and whispered to Janet, an adult worker in the nursery, "I think there's a bomb in the other room. I'm going to check to see, but in the meantime, get these kids out of here and alert our security guard." She thrust Kathy into Janet's arm. "I hope I'm wrong, but the backpack is the same type I found at IFI. Call 9-1-1."

As the two adults carried the youngest children and herded the ones who could walk into the hallway, Beth dashed back into the changing room and, with shaky hands, unzipped the bag. She looked inside, her gaze glued to the countdown.

Two minutes, fifty seconds.

No time to get the bomb squad here or possibly get everyone outside.

Instead, she had to take the bomb outside into the field behind the church. Still aware of the last few children moving into the hallway with Janet, Beth raced toward the door that led to the recreation area and across it to the chain-link fence around the playground. After slinging the bag over her shoulder, she scrambled over the fence, then flat out ran to the middle of the pasture. After laying it on the ground, she raced toward the parking lot.

People poured from the church.

Beth waved her arms and shouted, "Stay back."

The blast of the explosion rocked Beth's world. She flew forward, crashing into the edge of the asphalt parking area. Through the haze in her mind, the sound of sirens rang, and then blackness swallowed her.

* * *

Colby drove as fast as he could to make it

to the church before the service started. When he went to bed last night, he'd decided to set his alarm and try to make the last service and luncheon as a surprise for Nana and Beth. But he'd slept through his alarm. Knowing his grandmother and Beth, they probably thought he needed the rest and decided not to disturb him.

Nearing the church, a loud noise reverberated through the air as though a bomb had detonated. A plume of dark smoke shot up into the sky—in the direction of the church.

His cell phone went off—a call from his captain. "Colby Parker here."

"A bomb exploded at The Redeemer Church. You and Duke are needed there."

"Any casualties?" he asked as he made a U-turn.

"Don't know for sure."

Colby floored the accelerator as the fire trucks and police cars headed in the opposite direction. He raced into Nana's house and got what he should take: Duke, his leash, and Colby's gun and badge. Then he retraced his route to the church, shaken by the similarity to what happened to Kelly at the bank.

Please, Lord, let there be no casualties. I know I haven't been the best Christian in years, but I don't want anything to happen to the people I care about—especially Nana…Beth. I can't go through another woman I care about dying because I slept through my alarm.

He parked behind a police vehicle, put the leash on Duke and headed for the senior officer at the church. Out of the corner of his eye, he spied a group. His grandmother was part of it. They stood around a woman lying on the ground at the back of the parking lot. He headed there. Behind the group were firefighters spraying water on the field. As he drew nearer, he stared at the hole the bomb had created.

Colby neared the crowd as an ambulance pulled into the parking lot. When the people parted to allow the EMTs close to the injured person, Colby glimpsed the victim and came to a halt as he stared at Beth on the ground.

Colby's heartbeat pounded through his

body. What happened here?

As the paramedics checked Beth, Nana approached him. "She'll be all right. She hit the pavement hard from the blast, but it doesn't look like she was hit by any shrapnel. He moved closer as the others standing around Beth stepped back further. The EMTs carefully turned her over.

Her left cheek and arm were scraped. Pain, she was trying to control, twisted the features of her face. Her gaze caught his. A brief gleam lit her eyes until the paramedics transferred her to the gurney. She moaned.

"I'm going to find this bomber." Colby gave Duke the signal to stay put then held her right hand as she was rolled to the ambulance nearby. "What happened?" He pointed toward the field and raised his voice, realizing she might not hear what he was saying if her ears were ringing from the blast. He hated asking her at this time, but he needed as much information as he could about the bomb and how she came to be so close to it.

"The backpack was in the nursery's

changing room."

While one of the EMTs hopped up into the back with Beth, she struggled to raise her head and stared at Colby. "The other volunteers in the nursery got the kids out of the church and alerted the security guard about the possibility of a bomb." She tried to draw in a deep breath and grimaced.

The paramedic said, "We need to get her to the hospital."

"Not yet." Gently, Beth laid her head back on the gurney.

Colby climbed into the rear next to her, holding her hand. "I'll come to the hospital later and get the rest of your statement." Then he turned to leave.

"No. Need to find the bomber. I checked the bag and saw the timer with two minutes fifty seconds on it. I knew it would go off before everyone was out of the building, so I took it out of the building. I don't know how the backpack got into the nursery. Find out." The last few words came out in a soft, pain-filled voice as though all her energy siphoned from her.

"I will." With a nod, Colby jumped down from the ambulance and closed the doors, signaling Duke to come to him.

His muscles tightened in the pit of his stomach while his hands fisted. Had Carson planted this bomb prior to his death? Or was the other guy who stayed at his apartment at The Village finishing the job. Had the bombs been Carson's way to go after Beth? What if Beth had been the target all along, and the rug gallery and the grocery store had been a diversion? The police might never discover the reason behind the bombs even if they caught the other guy.

Nana approached Colby. "What did Beth say?"

He quickly told her while holding Duke's leash. "Is the nursery used before Beth goes into work?"

"Yes. During the first service and the Sunday school classes. She works the late service."

"Thanks. Show me where she would have left the nursery. It would have been the nearest exit."

His grandma took him to the opposite side of the church and gestured toward the playground and the exit within a fenced yard. Colby went to the gate and noted it was locked. "Did Beth have a key for the lock?"

"No. She must have climbed over. The fence is only four feet to keep the kids inside."

"Will you go to the hospital and keep me informed about what's going on? I need to find the person who did this."

"Of course, I will."

He nodded and turned away from the playground. "Where's the nearest unlocked door I can use to get inside?"

Nana walked around the building toward a side door into the church. "I'll need the key to her car to drive it to the hospital. It's in her handbag in the nursery. I'm sure she'll want her bag anyway."

"Where is it?"

"In the cabinet, top shelf, on the right of the main door in her nursery. That's where the volunteers keep their purses."

Colby reached the nursery and found

Beth's bag. He handed it to Nana, who retrieved the car keys. "Don't forget to call when you know something about Beth. Oh, and if you see the security person, tell him I need to see him."

"That's Bud Dawson. He's probably in the office looking at the video footage."

"Show me the way to the office. I need to get that footage."

He followed his grandma to where Dawson was. Then she left so Colby could talk to Bud. "Have you pulled up the video footage covering the church?"

"No, I just came here. I talked with Captain McHenry when he arrived. He'll be in here for the video footage."

"I noticed there's a camera in the nursery where the bomb was. Can you pull that up?"

"Sure." Dawson sat in front of the computer and brought up the program. He clicked on it and a black screen came up. "Something's wrong. It's not working in the nursery." Then the security guard tried a couple of other cameras. They were blank, too. "Someone took down our surveillance cameras."

Captain McHenry entered. "We don't have any video footage?"

"None. Captain, I'm going to take Duke through the whole building to make sure there isn't a second bomb." Colby walked through the group of offices before he headed down the hall.

He didn't think there was another bomb because that hadn't been the case so far. He wanted to be at the hospital with Beth. She had saved many lives. With all that happened in the past few days, they now knew there was more than one person involved in the bombings. Who was Carson's partner? His mysterious visitor?

* * *

The sound of an explosion reverberated through her mind, startling Beth awake. Her eyes popped open. She sat forward, flinging her right arm out and connecting with the rolling table.

Pain from her sudden movement pounded against Beth's skull and chest, demanding her attention. Not only did she have a concussion but also scrapes down the left side of her body and bruised ribs. She would be staying at the hospital at least overnight. Still, she would do what she'd done again if necessary. No one was injured or killed in the attempt to bomb the church. That thought gave her comfort in the midst of the anguish.

She tried to reach for her water, ground her teeth, and finally grasped the plastic cup. After sipping the cool liquid, she again leaned toward the table to put her mug down. She groaned.

A light knock sounded at the door right before a young man dressed in blue scrubs with a hospital lanyard around his neck came into the room. "I'm Brian, an orderly on this floor. Is there anything I can help you with?" He had brown hair and eyes with a pleasing face in spite of a two-inch scar on his left cheek.

"Yes, please bring the rolling table closer and lock it in place so it won't move. Also, I need more water."

Brian took her plastic pitcher and filled

it with water, then placed it where she could reach it easily. "Anything else?"

"No. Thanks." Beth closed her eyes, the brief effort she'd exerted draining her energy.

"Call the nurses' station if you need any other help." The orderly pointed to the button on the side of the bed when Beth's eyelids slowly lifted.

The door swung open, and Ann hurried into her room, halting when she spied the orderly.

He nodded his head toward Ann and left the room.

"I was gone only ten minutes. Did you need help?" Ann took the chair near the bed and sat.

"I was having a battle with the rolling table. Brian took care of it. Do you know what's going on at the church?"

"There was only one bomb. Someone hacked into the computer and turned off the security cameras last night."

"Was the bomb planted in the nursery last night? After Thomas was killed?"

"Maybe. No one knows for sure. They're

looking for any video footage from places around the church, but I don't want you to worry."

Beth stared at the wall across from the bed at the clock. Six-seventeen. "How's Colby?"

"He called a few times to see how you were doing. I haven't heard from him in a couple of hours. The town is crawling with FBI and ATF officers. They're looking for the person who visited Thomas. They ran his fingerprints, obtained at the cabin not far from where Thomas was killed. Now the authorities have a picture of him, and it's been plastered all over the media. Thomas's fingerprints were at the cabin too. They had to be working together."

"Who is the other man?"

"Brett Johnson. It's only a matter of time before he's spotted."

Beth closed her eyes for a moment. "Thank God this will come to an end soon."

"I hope so."

"I hope everyone is all right at the church, especially the kids in the nursery."

Ann took the chair next to Beth's bed.

"There won't be any phone calls coming into your room."

"What's going on?"

"You know what happened after the bus wreck. You were on the news because you went back into the burning bus to get Clara. The media frenzy is happening again, but this time, I think it'll be even worse. The video of you running with the bomb bag into the field by the church went viral. One of the parishioners filmed it on his cell phone."

"Thanks. I don't want to deal with that again. I did what needed to be done."

A knock on the door startled Beth. She tensed and immediately regretted doing that. "Come in," she said, trying to relax as much as she could—which wasn't a lot. A bomber was still out there, and she'd been personally targeted by his placement of the bombs. With Thomas being involved somehow, she wasn't surprised the targets were connected to her—at least two of them directly—but she often shopped at the grocery store.

The door opened.

Beth homed in on who entered. Her jaw dropped. In the years since she'd left home, the only way she could see her parents was to travel to them. The way they left home was to move to a new one. This surprised her, but she was so glad her mother was here. "Mom, how did you get here? Is Dad with you?"

"No. He couldn't come." Her mom took the chair next to Ann.

"And he let you drive five hours by yourself. Why?"

"He had his reasons, and I'm perfectly capable of driving a car for longer than that."

This didn't feel right. "What are you not telling me? I have to get hurt to get you to finally come see me. You always had an excuse for why you or Dad couldn't come visit." Feelings she'd questioned for years flooded Beth. She studied her mother who looked down at her hands in her lap then to Ann. Her mom wasn't looking at her. Something was wrong beyond Beth and her injury.

Colby's grandma rose. "I'll leave you

two to talk. I have calls to make to people at church."

"Okay. She's gone, Mom. What are you keeping from me? Are you and Dad separated? Is something wrong with him?"

She lifted her head and stared at Beth. "We did have a fight."

"Why? What about?"

"Married people disagree from time to time."

She's hiding something from me. "Mom, I want the truth."

Her mother sighed and looked right at Beth. She started to say something but snapped her mouth closed.

THIRTEEN

A tear ran down Beth's cheek, and she turned her head away from the woman she'd looked up to all her life. "Mom, go home."

"Beth, your dad and I have always tried to protect you. That has been paramount to us. I wouldn't change what I've done to insure you're safe."

Fear stared back at Beth. "What have you done?"

Silence hung in the air for a long moment. "What I'm telling you, you can't tell anyone. It will put me and your dad in danger."

"Danger!" Beth sat forward, pain

stabbing her chest at her sudden move. "How? Because of what I did? The police have caught one bomber and are narrowing in on the other one."

Her mother drew in a deep breath then slowly released it. "When you were three years old, your dad testified against his boss, and the man went to prison. We had to go into the Witness Protection Program. Your dad didn't want you to know that he'd been an accountant for a crime organization. When he first took the job, he didn't know that about his employer. We became friends with his boss and his wife. Over time, your dad realized his employer was crooked. He was afraid to say anything, especially when he learned how dangerous the guy was. Then the FBI arrested your dad. With his testimony, A.C. Slater was convicted and sent to prison. We were relocated. Your dad could never live in one place for more than a couple of years although the U.S. Marshal assigned to his case assured him everything was all right. Your father kept moving us because if anything happened to you and me, he would never forgive himself for putting us in harm's way."

Tears flooded Beth's eyes. She squeezed them closed, but a wet trail coursed down her cheeks.

Her mother, who looked so much like her, took her hand and held it between hers. "We didn't want you to worry about the people who wanted to make your dad pay for his testimony."

Beth tugged her hand away and swiped her cheeks. "Then you shouldn't be here now. I don't want to be responsible for something happening to you or Dad."

"Hon, the good thing is, A.C. Slater died in prison last month. I think we're safe, but your dad's still worried. I knew I couldn't keep myself from coming here. Not when you were hurt. When I left, I asked your father to contact the U.S. Marshal in charge of our case and see what he thought about our danger threat. I hope your dad will join us."

"Is that why you never had another child?"

"Yes. We couldn't take the chance. I

know how much you wanted a sister or even a brother. I wanted more children, but the risk was too much. A. C. Slater was a monster. Your dad didn't know any of that until he was in too deep."

The pain in her head intensified with all that she'd learned. Now she understood the restrictions her parents had insisted on, like no online accounts. The kids she spent time with were checked out by her father. She never got to go to summer camp or spend the night at a friend's house. "So that's why I had a cell phone before any of my friends."

"Yes, we needed to know where you were at all time."

Beth leaned back against the bed and tried to relax. Tensing only hurt her more. For years her parents never told her the truth. Yes, for her well-being in their eyes, but they should have told her at least when she was an adult. She had a right to know. *How can I forgive them?*

* * *

KIDNAPPED

"Nana, how is Beth?" Colby parked behind a police vehicle near a warehouse where the authorities suspected that Carson's partner was holed up—at least that was what their reliable tip said.

"She got a surprise visitor today."

"Who?" Colby exited his truck and opened the back door to let Duke out.

"Her mother. Even before Beth said anything, I knew it was her mom. They look a lot alike."

He clipped the leash on Duke's halter. "I wanted to call her parents, but I didn't have a way of getting in touch with them. Did Beth call her?"

"No, her mother heard on the news and drove here. I left to give Beth some alone time with her mom. She'll stay with Beth tonight, so I'll be going home in a little while."

"I've got to go. We're near apprehending the other person involved in the bombings. I'll be at the hospital when I can." He needed to see with his own eyes that Beth would be all right. In one week, he'd come to care about her. He told her he'd protect her. He didn't want anything to happen to her. "I'll see you at home later."

"I'll be praying for you and the other police officers."

"Thanks. We need that. Bye." As he said that to Nana, he realized he meant every word. His anger at the Lord had denied him a chance to get past his pain, sorrow, and wrath at what happened to Kelly. He'd forgotten how to pray. Being with his grandma—and Beth—helped him to remember the need.

He disconnected his call, pocketed his cell phone, then hurried toward the leader of the bomb squad. They had to go in first in case the warehouse was rigged with a bomb to explode. Colby with Duke and the two ATF bomb-sniffing canine teams would follow quickly behind them. It was likely that Carson's partner still carried the scent of the bombs he made and used. Since Duke was a vapor-wake canine, he could track the suspect's movements through the warehouse faster. That was their mission while the bomb squad and ATF canines made sure the place didn't have any bomb set to go off.

As Colby and Duke entered the warehouse, his dog pulled to the left immediately. Colby gave him a long leash. Duke weaved his way through the first floor until he reached the stairs to the second level. They climbed the steps. Big boxes were stacked along the south and west walls. But his dog didn't go in that direction. He headed right, stopped in front of a closed door, and sat. Colby drew his gun and stood off to the side of the entrance into the room. Colby signaled to Duke to move to him and stay.

With his hand on the knob, he turned it, pushed the door open, and ducked away from the entrance. Nothing happened. Colby charged inside, gun clasped in both his hands. His gaze swept the area, empty except for a desk and chair in the middle. He checked the furniture. Nothing.

"Duke, come." When his canine entered, Colby gave the sign to search.

His dog stopped and pointed his nose up toward the ceiling. Quietly, Colby climbed up on the desk and with his left hand, lifted the ceiling tile while pointing his gun with his right one. A shot flew by Colby's head, grazing his scalp. He returned fire as the man tried to crawl away. The suspect's weight caused the tile to collapse, and he fell to the floor. As Colby jumped down from the desk, Duke attacked the man who was trying to get up. Colby quickly turned him over and handcuffed his hands behind him.

As he led the second bomber down the stairs to the first floor, Duke walked beside him, his attention focused on the target. The man, whose prints were found at the cabin near the bomb site where Carson was killed and identified as Brett Johnson, was passed off to two police officers to escort to headquarters.

"Good work." The leader of the bomb squad stopped next to Colby. "You need a paramedic to take a look at your wound."

His adrenaline had been so high, Colby hadn't felt the pain. He touched the spot on the side of his head. When he looked at his hand, blood covered his fingers. "Will do."

After he was attended to, he drove to

the hospital, per the medic's strong suggestion, where Colby had stitches before he went to the third floor where Beth was. He needed to see she would be all right and to tell her the last bomber had been apprehended.

* * *

"So, can you and Dad live a normal life now that A. C. Slater is dead?" Beth finally asked after sitting in silence in her hospital room with her mother.

Her mom sat forward. "We live a normal, quiet life. We like it. That won't change because A. C. Slater died."

"Will you still move around every two years? I always hated that." As a child, she kept that to herself, but she wasn't going to do it ever again.

"I don't know. I'd love to move here or somewhere closer to you. All of this has just happened. We've lived under this stress and fear for over twenty-four years. We didn't want that for you too."

Neither did she—for her parents. "Why

didn't you tell me when I was older?"

"We'd kept the secret for so long we didn't want to say anything. Even with A. C. Slater's death, your dad wanted what happened in the past to stay there. He's a proud man and still hasn't forgiven himself for getting caught up in the mess all those years ago. We considered the Slaters our friends."

Beth fought to keep her anger from surfacing. Her parents, especially her father, all her life had stressed how important it was to tell the truth. And now she was finding out his life was a lie. "Where are you staying tonight?"

"Here, with you. A nurse on the floor said the lounge chair in this room nearly flattens out, and it's comfortable to sleep in. There's an extra pillow and blanket I can use. Unless you don't want me here."

"No, Mom. I'm glad you're here."

"Are you still upset with what I revealed?"

"I'm shocked and yes, still upset, but I'm glad you're here. The past week has had some real lows but also a few highs." A picture of Colby flitted through her mind. Where was he? She needed to see him.

"Have you eaten dinner yet?"

"No, but it'll be delivered soon."

"I saw a place downstairs where I can grab something to eat and bring it back to the room."

"That sounds good." Beth needed time to assimilate all her mother's news. "But you can take your time or even eat down there."

"I understand. I've dropped a lot in your lap today. I'll be back in half an hour." Her mother rose and walked to the exit. "I love you." Then she left, weariness in her expression.

As the door closed, so did Beth's eyes. So many emotions swirled around in her head. The vision of Colby haunted her. She wanted to talk to him about what her mother had told her, but her mother didn't want her to tell anyone.

While her mom was gone, she would call Colby. She struggled to sit up, ignoring the bruised ribs as much as she could, and leaned over to grab her cell phone on the end table next to the bed.

Her door opened, and Beth immediately swung her attention to the entrance. Colby. She relaxed against the bed, set at about a seventy-degree angle, and smiled. "It's good to see you." Alive with a bandage around his head. "How's the case going?"

"We caught Brett Johnson, the guy who'd visited Carson's apartment and stayed there. The man reeked with the scent of the bomb ingredients from the devices used in all the attacks. Duke found him in a warehouse where he'd been hiding."

She looked at Duke by Colby's side. "That's wonderful. He's one of the heroes. Come in both of you. Tell me how you knew where the guy was hiding. Also, what happened to your head?"

"I stopped in at the ER and had to get stitches, or I would have been here earlier. A bullet grazed me. What I want to know is how *you're* doing?" He took the chair where her mother had been.

"My mother's here. She heard what happened, hopped into the car, and drove to see how I was."

"Where is she?"

"Getting something to eat downstairs." She gestured toward the chair near her. "Tell me who the second bomber was?"

"Did Thomas Carson ever talk about a Brett Johnson?" He sat, signaling to Duke to lie down next to him.

"The name doesn't sound familiar."

Colby withdrew his cell phone and turned it on. "Anyone who looks like this?" He showed her the screen shot.

"No. That's the other guy?"

"Yes. Besides Carson's, the other fingerprints we found in the cabin were Brett Johnson's. We ran them through the database and that name came up. We think Johnson is the unknown guy staying with Carson. What little we knew of what he looked like from people who lived at The Village fits the guy's description."

"Any information on where he lived, worked?"

"A Dallas address was the last place. He hadn't lived there in two months. He was caught in a warehouse, but there was no indication he was living there. Once we had a photo of the second bomber, we got his picture out. A tip on his whereabouts came in on our hotline."

"Where does Thomas fit in with this?"

"Have you ever shopped at the bombed grocery store or the Prescott Rug Galley?"

"The grocery store." His question suddenly struck Beth, confirming something she had wondered. "You think I'm the connection?"

"It's a possibility. We may never know the reason behind why they chose those targets unless Johnson tells us. We're digging into his background. Maybe there are answers there as well as in Carson's past. There are some people who are so angry they just lash out."

She touched her hand to her right temple and massaged it. Her eyelids grew heavy. "I'm going to concentrate on healing and putting my life back together. I still want to get Gabe and my security system. When I'm better, I hope you'll teach me self-defense. I don't want to be caught off guard again."

"I will. When do you think you'll be released from the hospital?"

"Tomorrow, hopefully, early. I want to be at my place when the security company puts in my system in the afternoon. I imagine now with my mother here, she'll want to take me to my house. Will you let Ann know that?"

"Yes, and I'll come as soon as I'm off duty. I'll let Joe know you still want Gabe."

"Thanks." Seeing Colby lifted her spirits. Zeroing in on him kept her from focusing on her pain.

"At least things will settle down for you now. I'm glad…" His voice faded into silence as the door opened. He tensed, his gaze glued to her mother coming into the room.

"Mom, this is Colby Parker, a police officer who's been working on the bombing case. His bomb-sniffing dog is Duke." Beth gestured toward the Rottweiler whose ears perked forward when she said his name. "He's an amazing animal." As well as his owner, but she kept that quiet.

Her mother covered the distance between her and Colby. "I'm Mary

Sherman. I appreciate what you've done to help my daughter."

After he shook her mom's hand, Colby rose and indicated to Duke to do the same. "It's a pleasure to meet you. I understand you're going to stay with Beth tonight." He stepped away from the chair. "We need to leave. I have to stop by headquarters before going home." He caught Beth's attention. "I'll call you tomorrow. Good night."

When Colby left the room, Beth missed him immediately. In a week, she'd become dependent on him. She felt safe with him, which surprised her because she'd been so wrong about Thomas. She should be leery, but in her heart, she couldn't feel that way about Colby. She hoped she wasn't going to get her heart broken again.

* * *

Finally, Beth returned to her own house after a week at Ann's. Although Thomas was dead and couldn't survey her, she decided to go ahead with the security system installation she had scheduled for this afternoon. She'd talked with the office manager, and she gave her a range of time between three and five when the crew would arrive.

Her mother came into the kitchen where Beth sat at the table, staring out the bay window. "Dad sends his love. I told him I'm staying at least three or four days. If you need me longer, then I'll extend the time. Shouldn't you be lying down?"

"I will. I just got off the phone with Safe Security Company to make sure they're still coming."

"Good. I'll feel better once it's installed. When are you going to get Gabe? I hope while I'm here."

"I'll see Colby tonight and see what he thinks. It's his friend who has Gabe."

Beth yawned. "I think I'll lie down for a while. If I'm not up by the time the security company comes, wake me when they arrive."

Beth stood, gripping the edge of the kitchen table to steady herself. For a few seconds, the room spun. She had to remember she would need several days of recovery before she could get back to normal.

The doorbell rang.

"Honey, I'll get it. Go on and go to bed." Her mom left the kitchen.

As Beth came into the hallway that led to her bedroom, she glanced to the left.

Her mother held two large flower bouquets in a glass vase. "It looks like you have some people who really care about you. Where do you want them?"

"In the living room. Who sent them?"

"One is from IFI and Mr. Knight." She walked to the far end table next to the couch and put the two-dozen, white and red roses down then took the other vase with multi-varied flowers from carnations to lilies. "This is from Colby."

Her cheeks flushed as her mother studied her reaction. "I haven't had a chance to really get to know him, but I hope I can in the next few days."

Beth swung around before her whole face reddened like the roses in the far vase. "I'll see you in a couple of hours," she mumbled.

Beth eased onto the bed and slowly turned to lie down, trying not to twist her chest. But when the doorbell rang again, the noise startled her. She made a sudden movement and pain shot through her chest. She never realized how much bruised ribs could hurt.

Rest was what the doctor ordered, and she would follow those directions. She eased herself down onto the mattress, lying face up. Her heavy eyelids slid closed and sleep whisked her away…

A creaking sound nibbled at the edges of her consciousness. She didn't want to wake up, but someone stood nearby. She moved her hand toward the edge of the bed, her fingers contacting a jean clad leg. Colby?

Her eyes bolted open, and a man she'd never seen before stood over her.

FOURTEEN

Colby drove toward Beth's to make sure she was settled in her home. He wanted to confirm the security system was done the correct way. Several police officers he worked with said that Safe Security Company was an excellent one, but he wanted to see for himself. Beth had gone through enough in this past week. He also needed to see for himself she was all right.

Two blocks away, he received a call from the security company, and he answered it. "Sergeant Parker here."

"I'm Don Nickels from Safe Security Company. I'm at Ms. Sherman's house, and no one is answering the door. I've rung the bell and called her. We talked earlier today, and she said she would be here."

"I'm two minutes away. I'll be there." He disconnected that call and made another to Nana. He asked her to go to Beth's house and bring the spare key she'd given his grandma.

When Colby pulled into the driveway, his heartbeat thumped against his ribcage. He hopped out of his patrol SUV, let Duke out, and hurried to the porch where Don and his partner stood. Nana scurried across the neighbor's yard and arrived right after he did.

Colby took Beth's key from his grandma and inserted it into the lock. When he entered the house with his dog next to him, he shouted, "Beth, this is Colby."

Silence.

On the floor in the entry hall was a broken vase with flowers scattered everywhere as though someone had dropped the bouquet. A nearby small table in the foyer was knocked over.

Withdrawing his gun, Colby went to the

right through the living and dining rooms, keeping Duke by his side. As he moved into the kitchen, his gut solidified. He didn't have a good feeling about this. He opened the door to the garage. Beth's and her mom's cars were parked inside.

So, where were they?

The answers that popped into his mind churned his stomach. Could they have somehow missed a third person involved in the bombings? Each hour, more evidence had been discovered, but nothing about another partner being involved. Colby continued the search through the house. When he went into Beth's room, the spread and sheets were strewn on the floor as if she'd been yanked from the bed.

He called headquarters. "I believe Beth and Mary Sherman have been taken from Beth's home. There's evidence they didn't go willingly."

When Colby hung up, he headed back to the foyer and outside on the porch. He turned to his grandma and the two men from the security company. "Beth Sherman and her mother aren't here. It looks like someone took them. I have more officers coming."

What have I missed, Lord? Why did someone take Beth and her mother? I need Your help.

* * *

Beth opened her eyes to darkness. She tried to move. Her body protested with sharp pain shooting through her. Her chest burned as she fought against ropes across her torso. For a moment, panic attacked her, robbing her of oxygen. She gasped for a breath. Then another.

Lord, help!

"Beth, are you all right?"

The sound of her mother's voice eased the tension gripping her. "All I remember is being yanked from my bed. Then I felt a prick on my neck. After that, I must have blacked out."

"I thought the two men who came into the house were from the security company. The van they parked out front had Safe Security Company on its side. After a flower shop delivered another bouquet from your church, the two men came up to the porch. Before I could react, I was grabbed and knocked out with some kind of drug."

Sitting in a hardback wooden chair, Beth tugged on the ropes around her wrists, ignoring the pain zipping up her scraped left arm and through her chest. But she couldn't budge her shackles. The same with the cords around her ankles. "Is this tied to the bombing? I thought it was over."

For a long moment, her mother didn't say anything.

"Mom?"

"There's another possibility. I should have stayed away from you. This could be connected to A.C. Slater. I thought it would be over when he died. Maybe your dad was right."

"Or there are two other guys who helped Brett Johnson and Thomas." Exhaustion set in, and Beth tried to fight it. "Not knowing makes this even worse."

"We have to give this to the Lord."

Beth focused on the calmness in her

mother's voice. Freaking out would not help her. They needed to figure a way out of this. If only she knew where she was. What was outside this totally dark room?

* * *

While the forensic team gathered what clues might be in the house, Colby walked around Beth's bedroom to see if anything might have been taken besides her. He hoped some of the fingerprints on the door were a clue to who took her and her mother.

One of the crime scene investigators lifted the sheet and blanket on the floor and put them in a large plastic bag. Colby caught sight of a syringe partially under the bed. With gloves on, he bent down, picked up the syringe, and put it in an evidence bag. Then he checked what else might be under there. Nothing.

Captain McHenry stood in the entrance. "May I have a word with you?"

Colby straightened and headed into the hallway.

"We received a call from Safe Security Company earlier that one of their vans and two technicians were missing. The two men were found twenty minutes ago, dead in an alleyway. There was a camera that captured it all on tape. Several were disabled, but they missed the one across the street that had an angle on the alley. We tracked the van. We know from the GPS system in the vehicle that they came here."

"Any pictures of the killers?"

"We're accessing all cameras on the route they took. So far nothing on what the kidnappers look like. We found the empty van outside of town. There are no cameras we can access in that area. I thought you would like to be involved in the search with Duke. I have several other canine teams coming to see if we can find a trail to follow."

"Yes, sir. I found a syringe that most likely was used to immobilize Beth. I need to get Duke. He's out back."

After the captain gave him the location on the outskirts of Cimarron City, Colby hurried and retrieved Duke then made his way to his police SUV.

Two men were dead because they worked for the security company Beth had hired. They had come after Beth and her mother. He had to find them before they were murdered too if it wasn't already too late. Was there a chance they missed two other people involved in the bombings, or was there something else going on?

* * *

In spite of the pain, Beth continued to struggle with the ropes around her wrists. The back slats on the wooden chair creaked as she fought to free herself. What would happen if she rocked the chair until it fell against the floor? Could she break it up and free herself?

"Mom, we need to try and get loose. Our lives are on the line even if we don't know why."

"At this moment, the why isn't important. I see a faint light coming through behind you. Must be a window."

Beth twisted as much as she could to see what her mother saw. Even turning right and left, she couldn't see anything because there was a blind spot directly behind her, and the pain from her bruised ribs was like sharp knives stabbing her chest. "I'm not going down without a fight." She had to figure a way out.

Voices drifted to Beth, getting louder as they neared her.

"I wish Colby had a chance to show me some self-defense moves I might be able to use," she whispered.

The door swung open. Blinding brightness flooded her surroundings. Two men entered. The taller one flipped on the overhead light while the other slammed the door closed. From the brief glimpse she had of the area beyond the room, she thought she was in a cabin. By the lake outside of town? Or somewhere else? She didn't know how long she'd been out from the drug she'd been given.

Then she saw the orderly from the hospital and gasped. His gaze zeroed in on her. "Is your name really Brian?"

He smirked. "No, and I'm not an orderly."

"Why were you in my room yesterday?" She wanted answers to what was going on.

"I needed to find out if your parents would be coming to Cimarron City, so I planted a bug in your hospital room to see what we could find about where your parents were. Too bad for you the wrong one came," the fake orderly said in a mocking tone. "Mrs. Slater was shown your picture from the viral video of the church bus rescue and was positive you were a grown-up version of Lizzie Worth because you look so much like your mother." He waved his hand toward Beth's mom. "We were sent to see if that was the case."

"Enough explanation." The taller guy came toward her, blocking her view of the fake orderly. She tensed, balling her hands.

He grabbed her chin and jerked her head back. "Where is your dad? He's the one we're after."

Beth pressed her lips together. Now she knew why she'd been taken. She should have told Colby about A. C. Slater and the reason her family had been in witness protection.

The man narrowed his eyes and stared at her. He slapped the left side of her face, sending a wave of pain through her. She bit down on her lips, tasting her blood's metallic tang.

"I can keep doing this if you remain quiet. Where is your dad?"

Beth stiffened, preparing herself for another hit.

Instead, the fake orderly punched her mother in the stomach. Her mom struggled to breathe and bent over as far as she could with the ropes around her chest. "Where is your husband?"

"I—don't–know," her mother said between gasps for air.

The tall captor slapped Beth's left cheek again. It felt like his handprint was burned into her flesh. But she wouldn't react to it. She grinded her teeth together and glared at him.

Through the anger and pain, Beth heard her mother say, "We live in Bluebonnet, Texas. The address is 2340 Pine Street.

Don't hurt my daughter anymore. She has nothing to do with what happened to A.C. Slater."

"No, Mom," Beth screamed.

The fake orderly chuckled. "See that's not so hard to say."

The two kidnappers left the room.

Tears ran down Beth's face. How could her mother sell out Dad?

* * *

There was a good chance the two men who had taken Beth and her mother had another car they used after ditching the van. But Colby had Duke smell the rear area of the van where the women were probably kept. Two other canine teams were also checking the surrounding woods.

Colby clenched the leash and went east of the van. What he couldn't get out of his head was the possibility of finding Beth—dead. She'd told him once her parents lived in Bluebonnet, Texas. He'd called the police there to send a car to Mary Sherman's residence. He didn't know the father's first name.

"We got the ID of one of the men who took Beth and Mary Sherman." Captain McHenry's voice came over his com.

"Do you want me to return?" Colby asked.

"Yes, another canine team's arrived. They'll take your place. We haven't ruled out a connection between the kidnappings and the bombings."

"Has Beth's father gotten in touch?" Colby asked when he returned to the van where he found the captain.

"No. The police chief in Bluebonnet just called, and Ethan Sherman isn't home. His car's gone. They'll follow through on tracking his vehicle."

"Thank you." The police needed the public's help in finding the two assailants, especially the man who'd been identified on the video footage. "Who is the man on the camera?"

"Carl Wiseman. He's wanted in New York for murder and kidnapping."

Colby's heartbeat increased at the thought of getting hold of the murderous

KIDNAPPED

thug. Why would a criminal from New York be after Beth and her mom?

"We're getting his photo out everywhere. I sent it to you." Captain McHenry's cell phone rang, and he answered it.

As the captain turned around and walked away while talking to his caller, Colby studied the picture of Carl Wiseman, memorizing his face. Something about the guy bothered him—an ordinary person with brown hair and eyes, but a two-inch scar on his left side of his face transfixed him. Had he seen him before? So much had happened in the past thirty-six hours. What was he missing?

* * *

"Beth, I didn't give your father's location away. I'd never do that," her mother whispered.

"But you told him your address." Beth's head still rang with the hits. The room swirled before her eyes, and she closed them.

"Your dad left after the bomb went off yesterday. I don't know where he went. The last time I talked to him was right before our kidnappers came to the house. Did you notice the area beyond this room had lights on? It might be nighttime."

Which would make it harder for the cops to find them. "We have to get out of here. They'll realize Dad isn't at the address you told them. We can't wait to be rescued."

"I agree. That's why I told them our address to give us some time."

An idea flashed across Beth's mind. "Let's move closer and turn back to back. I might be able to untie your hands and you mine."

"We'll have to be as quiet as we can."

"Okay. We'll turn around then move backward toward each other."

As they slowly inched their chairs around as quietly as possible against a wooden floor, Beth had to remember to breathe. She kept holding the air in her lungs until they burned. She exhaled slowly. Finally, she and her mom were back to back. Then they began moving toward each other.

Halfway there, the sound of footsteps grew louder—coming toward them. Beth didn't stop but kept trying to get closer to her mother.

She halted when someone turned the doorknob.

FIFTEEN

Carl Wiseman's photo nagged at Colby while he waited for Captain McHenry to finish his phone call. Colby had seen the man recently but couldn't remember where. He bridged the distance between the captain and him. "Any news about Beth and her mother?"

"Yes. Beth's damaged cell phone was found on the side of the road that leads to Boomer Lake Estates on the other side of town. It survived being tossed from the vehicle. It hit the pavement but bounced into the grass. We were able to track its location. We know two men took them, and we have the identity of one of them. We're checking all the traffic and security cams in the area around where it was found."

"What do you want me to do?"

"Lead a search of Boomer Lake Estates. I've dispatched three K-9 units to help you. When I get any information on the vehicle they used after this van, I'll let you know. The teams will meet with you outside the estates. They'll be dressed in casual clothes. No identification to show they're police officers. One team for each area. We'll need something that holds Beth's scent."

"I'll get some clothes for the teams. Let me know if Ethan Sherman is found."

"Will do."

As Colby walked to his SUV, a sense of helplessness struck him. What if he couldn't find Beth and her mother in time? *Lord, please protect them. Guide me to them*.

He drove to his grandma's house to change into casual clothes while grabbing some of Beth's clothing she'd left at Nana's. Leaving his police SUV behind, he took his truck and pushed the speed limit. He arrived right behind one of the three search teams. That police officer had brought a map of the area. Colby divided the estates into four sections as the other two teams parked behind him. Each police officer and his canine went to their designated search area.

Colby's portion was at the back of the subdivision, nearest to Boomer Lake behind the houses on the right side of the street. As he walked down the sidewalk, his cell phone rang.

"Any news, Captain?"

"Yes. The car is an older blue Buick. It belongs to the Fists who live in Boomer Lake Estates. The address is 1857 Ashton Street."

"That's my area to search. I just got here."

"We called the house, but no one answered."

"How long ago?"

"Three minutes. Inform the rest of the team and have them focus on that street. I'll be trying to reach the home's owner at his job."

After disconnecting with the captain, Colby contacted each team then strolled down the street until he was near 1857 Ashton Street, his position hidden behind a hedge between the Fists' house and their neighbor's. The drapes were closed along the front of the home. He didn't have a good feeling about this.

* * *

The door to where Beth and her mother were opened slowly. As she stared at the entrance, Beth held her breath. When both captors entered, their eyebrows slashed downward, their dark eyes narrowed into fury, and their mouth set in a scowl. She finally blew out a long stream of air.

They had been caught.

"You can't escape." The larger man covered the area between them, followed by the fake orderly.

The towering, bulkier kidnapper, six and a half feet tall, picked up the chair Beth had painstakingly moved toward her mother. Behind Beth the shorter guy turned her mom's chair around. She and Beth could look at each other but with an additional yard further apart.

The massive abductor, obviously the one calling the shots, stepped back from her and swiveled his attention to her mother. "Where is your husband? I need you to contact him."

Her mom lifted her chin. "I can't. He's left our house for good. He tossed his cell phone. The only way I can talk to him is if he calls me on a pre-paid phone he bought that doesn't have GPS. He won't use it unless it's an absolute emergency."

"Well, that's a pity." The guy in charged pulled out a handgun with a silencer, whipped around, and shot Beth.

A scream ripped from her mother's throat while a bullet ripped through Beth.

* * *

For a moment, Colby studied the setup of the Fists' house. "I'm going to the right. Waters, you go to the left," he said to the K-9 officer closest to him. "We'll meet in the backyard." Colby turned to the other two officers. "One of you go interview whoever lives here," he gestured toward the next-door neighbor's house. "It looks like someone's home. See what you can find out about the owner of this place." He turned to the last officer. "Stay here and let us know if someone comes or goes from here."

Colby started forward with Duke beside him on a short leash while Waters moved out with his K-9 at the same time. Colby ascended the steps to the front door. He rang the bell, its loud sound reverberating throughout the place. He waited a minute then pushed the button again. Still no one answered. He tried the knob, but the front door was locked.

He left the porch and walked toward the right side of the home. The blinds on every window he passed were closed. No way to look inside. He continued his trek to the rear of the house. It wasn't fenced along the back. The yard sloped down a small hill. Not far away was Boomer Lake. In the distance, he noticed a few cabins near the water and some docks with buildings on them.

He headed for the deck and the rear door. Waters met him there.

"All the blinds closed?" Colby mounted the steps.

"Yes. Unless the occupants were on vacation, that's unusual."

Colby stopped at the back entrance, grasped the knob, and turned it. The door opened. "Police," he shouted.

Silence.

Colby signaled Waters to go to the left while he went to the right to search the home. Colby took Duke off his leash, signaled him to heel, then withdrew his gun. In his gut, he sensed something was wrong. Off the kitchen, he opened the door to the garage. It was empty. The two kidnappers still had the car, or they'd ditched it. If only the older car had GPS. Then maybe they could locate it and find Beth and her mother.

They cleared the first floor and climbed the stairs to the second one. A faint smell of decay drifted to Colby. He pointed Waters to go left. Colby headed right, the nauseating scent growing stronger.

KIDNAPPED

When he entered the master bedroom, the stench of death bombarded him. His gaze fell upon the elderly couple lying on the bed, their dried blood everywhere on the sheets and coverlet.

He didn't think this had anything to do with the two bombers. This was about something else. It bothered him that Beth's father was missing too. Was Beth and her mother's disappearance connected to Ethan Sherman's absence?

Colby glanced at the door as Waters came into the room. "I'm calling this in. Let's go downstairs. I don't want to contaminate the crime scene. We have the identity of one of the men, but there may be evidence of the second one."

Colby phoned Captain McHenry. After he told him about the dead couple, Mr. and Mrs. Fist, he asked, "Any sighting of the Buick?"

"No, not yet. But it was caught on camera taking the road to the west side of Boomer Lake."

"I need a forensic team to go through this house for any evidence to tie the husband and wife's deaths to the abduction of Beth and her mother. I'll leave Waters here. The rest of us will join the search of the west part of the lake."

* * *

The force of the shot and her reaction sent Beth's chair toppling to the floor. Pain radiated from the bullet hole in her shoulder. Blood flowed from the wound, making her light-headed. To keep from bleeding out, she pressed her injury into the floor. She tried to keep her focus on her mother.

The door opened and the fake orderly, who had briefly left, came into the room, but he hung back at the door.

The tall kidnapper stood over her mom, his fisted hands gripping her blouse. "If you don't tell me where your husband is, I'll shoot another of your daughter's limbs."

"I don't know where my husband is. I have no way to get a hold of him. If I did, believe me I would tell you. He would want me to save our daughter."

Her mother's voice became weak and caught on the words "our daughter." Her mom's agony tore at Beth, intensifying her anguish.

"Tough, lady. I don't believe you." The larger man swung around and began lifting his gun.

"Love you, Mom." *I'm in Your hands, Lord*.

He aimed his weapon at her leg. Beth tried to prepare herself. He squeezed the trigger, and the bullet struck the floor near her calf.

He glanced over his shoulder at her mother. "The next one will be in her leg." Then he looked at Beth. "On the count of three. One. Two…"

Hunched over from the chair she was tied to, her mom launched herself at the kidnapper who was intent on hurting Beth.

"Th—ree."

The gun flew from his hand at the sudden contact, and he stumbled forward.

* * *

Colby and Duke left with a group of officers

to the north of the parking lot near the marina on Boomer Lake. Each cabin and shed was checked. Half were occupied. Some people they talked to live permanently at the lake. Colby interviewed each resident who was at home, showing them the photo of the blue Buick and another of Carl Wiseman.

At the marina, Captain McHenry told Colby the car had been sighted earlier today going south on the highway that led to Cimarron City. The police knew that they had been in route to kidnap Beth and her mother. Which meant the Buick had been caught on a video cam coming and going from here. So where was it now?

The further away from the harbor the denser the trees and brush became, except for the area along the shoreline and the narrow gravel road to the homes around the lake. To the right, Colby caught sight of something blue buried in the thick greenery.

He signaled to a nearby officer, Brown. "I think I found the Buick."

They headed to the blue object,

creating their own path through the thicket to the Buick. He spied the license plate number and called the captain. "We have the Fists' Buick." Then he gave McHenry the location. "I'm going to see if Duke can track Beth's scent from here. Officer Brown will go with me. I'll keep you in the loop."

Colby put on latex gloves and opened the driver's side door. The interior was clean. He popped the trunk and checked it in case the kidnappers had left the women there. He held out one of Beth's shirts for Duke to smell as he had before they had started the search at the lake.

Duke didn't waste any time. He headed into thick vegetation that Colby noticed had been broken and smashed onto the ground. This was the way the kidnappers drove the vehicle to hide it.

As Officer Brown and he followed Duke, Colby called the captain to send backup. He hoped he could find Beth and her mother before they were harmed. Through the forest, he spied a cabin. Colby reined in the leash, so Duke wouldn't break out of the woods before Colby could assess the situation.

Hidden, he stood at the edge of foliage and scrutinized the best way to proceed. In the woods surrounding the cabin, Colby went to the right and quickly as possible circled the cabin while Officer Brown stayed and watched the front, their coms open to let the other know the best and safest way to cross unseen over the twenty yards to the home. As he passed the sides of the place, Colby noticed the shades were all pulled down.

When he returned to Officer Brown, he said, "I'm going in through the rear door. There's only one window on that side and ten feet separate the thick brush from the house. Once inside, I'll make my way to the front and unlock that door. I need you to make sure no one leaves by that exit."

He rounded the house to the back. When Colby and Duke approached the rear of the place, his dog scratched at the wood. Beth had to be inside. His main concern was whether she was dead or alive. He tried the knob.

"I'm going to have to pick the lock.

Duke indicates Beth's inside." Colby spoke low into his mic.

While Colby bent over and inserted his tools to open the door, the sound of a gun with a silencer reverberated through the air followed by a woman's scream. One of the lock picks dropped to the ground. He snatched it up and quickly managed to get inside while whispering to Officer Brown, "I'm inside and making my way to where you are." With his gun in hand and Duke at his side, Colby sneaked toward the front entrance while checking the place.

Feet away from the first door he came to, a woman's voice, laced with fear, said, "I don't know where my husband is. I have no way to get a hold of him. If I did, believe me, I would tell you. He would want me to save our daughter."

He rushed to let Officer Brown into the cabin.

He swung the front door open as a man in a room in the back said, "Tough, lady. I don't believe you."

"Love you, Mom."

Hearing the plea in Beth's voice laser-focused him on getting to her as he approached quickly but also quietly. At least he knew Beth and her mother were alive.

Then another shot rang through the air. His heartbeat pulsated against his skull.

"The next one will be in her leg. On the count of three. One. Two…"

Colby raced toward the room where the kidnappers were keeping Beth and her mom.

"Th—ree."

His adrenaline pumped through his body as he wrenched the door open. His gaze zeroed in on Beth on the floor with a large man falling toward her. As Colby leaped forward, Officer Brown charged the other assailant. The tall accoster blocked his view of Beth while Colby tried to reach for his gun. He landed on the man, grabbing him by his upper arm while twisting them both to the side of Beth.

The fleeting sight of the blood on the wooden floor near her fueled his determination—and his anger. As Colby scrambled to subdue the man and use his knees to pin his arms down against the body, his gun flew from his hand. He plowed his fist into the guy's jaw several times. The kidnapper tried to buck Colby off him, but Colby channeled every ounce of strength into keeping the abductor down. Colby attempted to reach for his gun and still control the big man. Colby couldn't.

"Duke, bring to me." He pointed at the gun.

His Rottweiler nosed it toward Colby until he could grab it and point it at the kidnapper. "How's the partner?" Colby asked Officer Brown without taking his eye off his charge.

"Got him."

A few seconds later, Captain McHenry entered the cabin with five officers. The moment two police officers took over watching the large guy, Colby turned his full attention to Beth. "We need a paramedic now."

"On the way," the captain said.

Colby began untying the rope around Beth's wrists while another officer took care of her feet and pulled the chair away. Colby scanned the bedroom, saw a pillow, and took the case off it. He used it to stop the bleeding.

His gaze locked with Beth's, her eyes filled with pain. "Help is on the way. You'll be all right."

"Help is here." She tried to smile, but it only lasted a second.

As two paramedics entered, Colby leaned close and whispered, "I'm here for you."

A tear ran down her cheek. "Thanks."

Colby had to stand back as Beth was attended to and prepared for transport to the hospital. There was still work to be done to find all the answers, but at least Beth and her mother were all right.

Thank You, Lord, for protecting her.

* * *

In another hospital room later that night, Beth squeezed her father's hand. "I'm so glad you're alive." She adjusted her bed to sit up more. After the operation on her shoulder, she'd slept for several hours. She felt better than she had earlier, except that she hadn't seen Colby since the ER room right before they took her into surgery. Her mom had been here with her since after the operation.

Her dad grinned. "Ditto, hon." He glanced at her mom. "I should have agreed to come instead of you leaving without letting me know until you were halfway to Cimarron City. I talked with the U.S. Marshal's office an hour ago, and they're looking into our options."

"I thought the threat was over with A.C. Slater's death. I had to see that Beth was all right with my own eyes. What did Bob say when you called him about what I did and what happened here?"

"Who is Bob?" Although Beth's head still throbbed from the bombing at the church, it was becoming more tolerable.

"He's the new U.S. Marshal assigned to us. Well, not exactly new. We've been with him for the past two years. He's here working with the police on the case against the two kidnappers."

A light knock at the door startled Beth as it swung open. Colby came into the room, tired circles under his eyes. He looked her way, and a smile graced his mouth. "How are you doing?"

"Much better than this morning. What's happening with the two men?"

"One is talking and making a deal." Colby shook hands with her dad. "It's nice to meet you, sir." He stood on the opposite side of the bed from her parents.

"Which one is talking?" Beth was surprised that one would.

"Carl Wiseman. He has information that can completely take down the Slater Crime Syndicate. A.C.'s wife, Gloria, took it over and has been quietly building it back up over the past few years. According to the New York Police Department and the FBI, this all happened after her only child, a son, died from an opiate overdose. Right before I left the station, the other kidnapper started talking too. Based on their testimony, Gloria Slater is being arrested right now in New York City."

"Good. I'm ready to get back to a dull,

routine life." Beth tried to adjust her position. When she moved the wrong way, a shaft of pain reminded her of her bruised ribs, even with the pain meds following her surgery. She winced. "Getting back to a routine might take a week or so." She looked at her mother and father. "You two need to get something to eat."

"I'll stay while you have dinner. The café downstairs serves good food, even at this late hour." Colby came around to the other side of the bed. "She'll be in good hands."

Her parents glanced at each other and nodded. "Thank you for all you've done," her mom said. "Beth shared with me about the bombings and how you protected her. We'll be back as soon as possible. I imagine you need to get some rest after the day you've had."

After they left, Colby took the nearest chair to Beth, scooting even closer to her. "Let me tell you a little secret: I don't ever want to repeat today."

She chuckled and pressed a hand against her torso. "Don't make me laugh. It hurts too much."

He took her hand and held it. "When I couldn't find you this morning, I was afraid I'd never see you again. That I'd let you down."

In spite of the pain from her bruised ribs, she turned toward him. "You never let me down. You came for me. Meeting you changed my life. I won't ever forget the support you gave me. What Thomas did months ago and again recently has caused me to question my ability to see a person truly. How did I get Thomas so wrong?"

"Some people are good at hiding their true nature for a short time, but I've found on my job it doesn't stay hidden long. While trying to find Thomas, I interviewed some of his coworkers. He had a fiery temperament and lately had become combative. A few wondered if he was on drugs." Colby cupped his other hand over the one that already held hers.

"Looking back at the times I was dating him, I realize I tried to pacify him and gave him the benefit of the doubt more than I should have. I wanted to find someone I could love. I'm twenty-seven, and I hoped to marry, have a family, and settle down in one place. Not like my childhood where I moved all the time."

"I came back here because Cimarron City had been my home for nineteen years. I visited Nana over the twelve years I was gone. The feeling that I should return never went away. But then I would go by the bank where Kelly was murdered and the guilt that I wasn't there to protect her swamped me all over again."

"What could you have done to change the outcome?"

* * *

Beth's question swirled around in his mind. Colby should have been able to stop the man. Protect the person he loved. Today he'd been able to save her, but he'd been plagued with thoughts that he wouldn't—like with Kelly.

Suddenly he realized he was putting Beth in the same category with Kelly. *Protect the person he loved*.

"Colby, are you all right?" Beth asked.

He blinked. "Yes. Just tired."

"So am I. We can talk tomorrow."

"I don't want to leave until your parents come back."

"I'm fine. I have a police guard outside the room."

"That's the least we could do until the police are satisfied you're safe."

"Has Brett Johnson shed any light on the bombings? Do you know how Thomas and he are connected? Did Brett Johnson kill Thomas at the lake?"

"We don't think so. From the evidence and the situation, it looks like Thomas made a mistake while handling a bomb. We discovered Johnson has been here for a month and worked for the cleaning company that the church and IFI used. We think that was how the bomb was planted. He and Liam Quinn grew up together and were part of a violent gang. Johnson evaded being arrested, but Quinn didn't. He went to prison. When he wanted to join the army, he used his connections to buy a new identity—Thomas Carson."

"Why did they do it? Was it because of me?"

"Johnson isn't talking much. But from what we're finding out about their past together, they were an angry, vicious duo who got back together. You aren't to blame. They are, no matter what reason they tell themselves concerning the bombings.

The door opened, and her parents entered the room.

Colby rose and started for the exit but stopped and said, "I'll leave you to talk. My grandma has an extra room if you want to stay with her rather than in a hotel."

"Mom, that's where I stayed when I was waiting to have the security system put in at my house. Ann is a wonderful hostess and a good friend."

Mary Sherman sat in the chair Colby had vacated. "But I don't want you left alone. I talked with a nurse on this floor, and they have a portable bed we can use."

Beth's dad sank down on the small couch and patted it. "And as you know, I can sleep anywhere."

"Okay. I'll be back tomorrow." Colby left her room and the hospital. He was tired as he'd told Beth, but he didn't know if he'd be able to sleep.

What could you have done to change the outcome?

He wasn't able to answer that question.

He slipped into his truck and drove out of the parking lot. Instead of turning right to go to Nana's, he went left. He ended up sitting in his vehicle staring at the bank where his life had changed twelve years ago.

He lived. Kelly died. If he'd been there, what could he have done? The bank robbers came in shooting. Kelly was shot immediately. He'd been told by survivors how fast it had happened. He had to acknowledge that there wasn't anything he could have done. He had to let go of the past. If he didn't, he could never move on and relish the present. Kelly would have wanted that.

I can't change the past. I can't predict the future. But I can live for the present.

What do I want?

KIDNAPPED

The vision of Beth popped into his mind. In a short time, he'd let down more guards with her than he had with people he'd known a long time. He'd been afraid to care, using Kelly as the reason. Trying to find Beth today and succeeding made him realize how much he cared about her. He wanted more from life than just existing, and Beth was part of that dream.

Was it possible to fall in love with a person in such a short time?

Nana would tell him yes. She said she'd loved his grandfather after their first date. They married within a month of meeting each other. Until his granddad died a couple of years ago, they had been married happily for fifty years. He wanted a family like his grandparents' and parents' had.

* * *

Sunday night, almost two weeks later, Beth sat in her quiet home with a top-notch security system and Gabe on the floor by her feet. She would go back to work for a few hours tomorrow and work half-days for the rest of the week. She scanned her living room. She looked forward to seeing her fellow workers at IFI who had sent her bouquets of flowers every day. Their scent saturated the room with a sweet smell.

Her mom and dad left a few hours ago, and she already missed them, but they would be all right now. Mrs. Slater was arrested, and with the information the two men gave about being hired to kill Beth's father, she wouldn't leave prison. There was no Slater family left, and her attempt to run her husband's organization had failed.

The doorbell rang. Beth rose and hurried toward the foyer. After checking through the peephole, she let Colby into the house. Earlier he'd walked his grandma home.

She smiled. They hadn't had much of a chance to talk alone since she'd been rescued. Her only outing after leaving the hospital had been to attend church today. Colby had joined her and her parents. He'd walked with her to the spot where the bomb went off. The area still hadn't been filled. In silence they stood and looked into the hole, holding each other's hands.

In that moment, she felt at peace—something she hadn't been sure she would ever feel again, but with the pastor's words today, not to worry about the future and to relish the present, and the comforting company of Colby, she knew she could be at peace with the Lord in her life.

"Come in. I'm glad you're here."

A gleam in his gray eyes caught the light like polished silver. "How could I resist the invitation?" He moved toward the living room.

They sat next to each other on the couch. After petting Gabe, Colby slid his arm along the back while Beth cuddled close to him, pressed against his side. She felt as though she'd come home. In the past three weeks since meeting him, everything had shifted, and in the middle of those changes, she was falling in love with Colby.

"I'm glad you didn't resist. It's been so hectic. I finally feel like I can take a deep breath both for physical and mental reasons. Thankfully my bruised ribs are healing, and the bad guys are locked up or dead."

He brought his free hand up to cup her face. "That night in the hospital room you asked me what I could have done to change the outcome of Kelly's death. I went to the bank and sat in their parking lot while I tried to come up with an answer. I was scared to care for another woman after what happened to Kelly. But I discovered not caring was even scarier. When I was hunting for you, I realized that I didn't want to face a life without you. I want to see where this goes."

"What is 'this'?"

"Love."

She grinned. "Good because that's what I've been thinking. I'm falling in love with you and want you in my life too."

He leaned forward and brushed his lips over hers. When he deepened the kiss, she embraced him with her good arm while pressing closer to him. "You've given me a new life," he whispered against her mouth.

"I love how we think alike."

Chapter Excerpt from
HUNTED
Book one in the Everyday Heroes Series

ONE

Luke Michaels lay in his sleeping bag, hovering between consciousness and a dream state. A low growl yanked him wide awake. He sat straight up, still in a cocoon of warmth. Another deep rumble from Shep alerted Luke to possible danger. His German shepherd was nearby. He freed himself from his confines and scrambled to his feet.

Fearing a bear, Luke grabbed his rifle and hurried from his tent in the hills along the Kentucky River. He searched for his dog in the surrounding woods and spied him standing on a boulder overlooking the water. Tense. Alert.

In the early dawn, Luke scanned the terrain as he made his way to Shep. So focused on something in the distance, his dog didn't even acknowledge Luke's presence. He knelt next to his black and brown German shepherd and looked in the direction his dog stared.

What Luke saw chilled him in the warmth of a summer morning—a woman struggled to free herself from two men on the bridge. One guy slammed a fist into her jaw, and she went limp.

"Stay."

Barefooted, Luke plowed into the dense brush along the river, moving as fast as he could toward the trio a couple hundred yards away. Something sharp pierced the sole of his foot. He couldn't stop to see what. He kept going. His gaze shifted from the terrain to the two thugs hoisting her over the side.

Chains bound her.

Heart pounding, he stopped and raised his rifle, but before he could get off a shot, the assailants let her go. Too late.

HUNTED Excerpt

She splashed into the water and sank below.

Quickly, the two men disappeared from the side of the bridge. Clutching his rifle, Luke kept an eye on where she went into the river and raced as fast as he could nearer the location. He stopped on the bank closest to the area where she went under, laid his rifle down, and waded out into the cool water. He swam in the direction he thought she'd be, hoping she was still alive. The chains must have taken her to the bottom of the river. The very thought spurred him faster until he reached the spot. He dove down. The murky river limited his vision. He searched, sweeping his arms in front of him.

He didn't want to add her death to the others he hadn't been able to save. He surfaced, drew in a deep breath, then went back down. His lungs hurt. Would she even be alive if he found her?

He turned to swim up for another fortifying gulp of air when his foot brushed against something. He twisted back and felt around the muddy river. His hand encountered an arm. He couldn't waste any time bringing her to the surface.

Lungs burning, he clasped her under the arms and shot upward, her chain-clad body slowing his ascent. But he poured all his energy into kicking his legs. Finally, he broke through the surface, gulping in precious breaths while keeping her head above the water, pressing it against his as he swam for the shore a hundred feet away. He couldn't help her until he got her on land.

He dragged her out of the river and placed her on the ground. Thick chains bound her from her chest to below her knees. After he shoved them down her torso as much as he could, he immediately began chest compressions. He glanced at her beautiful face framed by shoulder length dark blonde hair.

"Live!"

She stirred, coughing and turning her head as water flowed from her mouth. Luke supported her upper body as she continued to clear her lungs. His gaze traveled down her body to assess for injuries. It was hard to tell with the shackles restraining arm and leg movement, but he didn't see any blood, except her lips where one of the men had struck her.

Finally, the woman stopped coughing and sank against his embrace, her eyelids fluttering. He pressed two fingers against her neck. Her racing pulse didn't surprise him after what she'd gone through.

"I'm Luke Michaels. Do you hurt anywhere?"

She opened her eyes, and for a few seconds, their crystalline blue color trapped him in a stare.

"No." She tried to sit up but collapsed back against him. "Yes." She drew in a breath then coughed again. "Hurt—all over."

He placed her gently on the ground. "Let me see if I can get these chains off you."

"Thanks," she murmured in a weak, raspy voice.

He tugged on the restraints, but the two padlocks holding the manacles around her remained tightly closed. "I need to take you back to my tent. I might be able to pick the locks." He looked up at the bridge—no sight of the two men. "Besides, I don't think this is a safe place to stay."

She rolled her head to the side to glance toward the bridge. "What happened?"

"Two men threw you off the bridge."

"Why?"

"You don't know?"

"No...I don't." She closed her eyes.

For a few seconds, he thought she'd passed out, but when she fixed her gaze on his face, he released a long sigh. "What do you remember?"

"Waking up—in the trunk of a car." She paused, her chest rising and falling rapidly as she sucked in shallow breaths. Panic took over her expression. Her eyes grew huge and flitted from one area to another.

Luke leaned into her line of vision. "Let's get you out of here. You're safe now." After slinging his rifle across his back, he worked his arms under her body then struggled to his feet, which painfully reminded him he'd stepped on something earlier. "My camp isn't too far from here."

While the lady rested her head against his shoulder, he retraced his path, limping the whole way back to Shep. His dog had stayed where he'd told him. Stopping near his German shepherd, Luke looked him in the eye. "Good boy. Alert."

The woman stared up at Luke. "Alert? You think those men will come here?" She tensed, fear invading her features.

"Alert is one of Shep's commands to stand guard. We're a team. We do a lot of search and rescue."

Her brows knitted together. "You were looking for me?"

"No. I like to go camping when I can get away. I was asleep when Shep alerted me that something was happening on the bridge." Luke ducked through the opening in the tent and laid her on his sleeping bag. "What's your name?"

He moved to his backpack and rummaged through it until he found his Swiss Army knife. While he went to work on the first padlock, she remained silent. After opening the lock and removing part of her chains, he glanced up to find her eyes clouded, her eyebrows scrunched. "Do you know who you are?"

"Sure," she said slowly. "I'm..." Her gaze slid away from his face.

He'd once rescued a couple of people who didn't remember anything about what had happened to them. Was she traumatized so much by what had occurred that she didn't even recall her name? After what he saw, it wouldn't surprise him if she had. He continued to work, turning his attention to the second lock. She would be sore and bruised from the shackles.

As he released the last restraints from around her, she murmured, "Megan Witherspoon. All I remember is two guys dragging me out of a trunk to the side of the bridge."

"So, you have no idea how you got into the trunk?"

Megan shook her head.

"Do you know the two men?"

"I don't think so. I only remember seeing one of them. The other was behind me."

HUNTED Excerpt

"What did he look like?"

"He's tall and husky. Like a body builder." Kneading the back of her neck, she stared at a spot on the tent above her. "Short dark hair—no, not short but pulled back." She looked at Luke. "I think it's long, but I'm not sure. And his eyes were so dark I thought they were black."

"Where do you live?" he asked as Megan, clad in wet jeans and a hot pink T-shirt, stretched her arms and legs as though making sure they worked before she struggled to sit up. He immediately assisted her.

"Sweetwater City."

"That's twenty miles from here. Is that where they grabbed you?" Luke reached for his duffel bag and pulled it toward him.

"I—I think so." Another series of coughs racked her body, her eyes watering from the exertion.

"When that guy hit you, he cut your lip." He picked up a cloth and pressed it against her wound.

"Thanks." She took the towel and held it against her mouth.

"You need to report this to the police."

"No!" She let her hand drop away from her face. "I don't know why someone tried to kill me. All I can remember is leaving my house to run errands." Her voice quavered. "After that, nothing—until I woke up in the trunk." Frustration dominated her expression as she massaged her temples.

Why would that keep her from reporting her abduction to the authorities? "But surely the police—"

"No. Those men think they killed me. How can I protect myself if I suddenly turn up alive, especially when I'm not sure what happened or what one of them looks like?" Shivering, Megan hugged her arms.

"Nothing needs to be decided right now. You're soaking wet. I have a pair of sweat pants and a T-shirt you can put on."

"That sounds wonderful." When she smiled, her blue eyes lit as though the sun shone through them.

He rummaged through his backpack, pulling out each article of clothing. "Not quite your size but dry."

"I'll make it work." Her gaze fixed on

his left foot. "You're bleeding." She gestured toward the cut.

He turned to the duffel bag and withdrew his first aid kit. "This is what happens when you run through the woods barefooted. It's nothing."

"It doesn't look like nothing to me. I can take care of it."

He started to tell her not to worry, but the concern on her face warmed his heart.

"It's the least I can do for you."

"I appreciate it." He handed her the kit and sat so his left foot was near her.

She laid his foot on her thigh then went to work, cleaning the injury then wrapping it in gauze. "You should get a tetanus shot and possibly have stitches."

"I had a tetanus shot earlier this year." Her gentle touch soothed the throbbing pain. "It looks like you've done this many times."

"I've worked with children. There. I'm done."

He started to say more, but fear and weariness carved deep lines into her face. After putting the first aid kit away, he put on his shoes and socks then stood, smiling. "Thanks." He headed for the tent opening. "While you change, I'll make breakfast and a pot of coffee. Come out when you're ready."

As Luke left Megan, one question came to the foreground. She couldn't have been running errands today because it was six o'clock in the morning. So, when was she kidnapped? His mind raced with hundreds of scenarios that could have landed her in this predicament. If only she remembered where she'd been, when she was there, and what made two men abduct her. The not knowing could definitely get her killed.

Books in the EVERYDAY HEROES Series

HUNTED, Book One

Murder. On the Run. Second Chances.

Luke Michaels' relaxing camping trip ends when he witnesses a woman being thrown from a bridge. He dives into the river to save her, shocked to find her wrapped in chains. As a canine search and rescue volunteer, Luke has assisted many victims, but never a beauty whose defeated gaze ignites his primal urge to protect. When Megan Witherspoon's killers make it clear they won't stop, Luke fights to save her, but can he keep her alive long enough to find out who is after her?

OBSESSED, Book Two

Stalker. Arson. Murder.

When a stalker ruthlessly targets people she loves, a woman flees her old life, creating a new identity as Serena Remington. Her plan to escape the madman and lead him away from family and friends worked for three years. Now he's back. With nowhere else to run, her only choice is war. Quinn Taylor, her neighbor and a firefighter with expertise in arson, comes to her aid, but will it be in time to save her?

TRAPPED, Book Three

Abduction. Death. Second chances.

When Beth Sherman interrupts a break-in at her house, her life changes drastically. When K9 police officer, Colby Parker, returns to his hometown after years of staying away, he finally must face his feelings concerning the murder of his fiancée.

Circumstances throw Beth and Colby together when a person leaves bombs in different public places around Cimarron City. They both have given up on love, but caught up in the dangerous situation, the pair find themselves falling in love. But can it last, especially when Beth is kidnapped?

Books in the STRONG WOMEN, EXTRAORDINARY SITUATIONS Series

DEADLY HUNT, Book One

All bodyguard Tess Miller wants is a vacation. But when a wounded stranger stumbles into her isolated cabin in the Arizona mountains, Tess becomes his lifeline. When Shane Burkhart opens his eyes, all he can focus on is his guardian angel leaning over him. And in the days to come he will need a guardian angel while being hunted by someone who wants him dead.

DEADLY INTENT, Book Two

Texas Ranger Sarah Osborn thought she would never see her high school sweetheart, Ian O'Leary, again. But fifteen years later, Ian, an ex-FBI agent, has someone targeting him, and she's assigned to the case. Can Sarah protect Ian and her heart?

DEADLY HOLIDAY, Book Three

Tory Caldwell witnesses a hit-and-run, but when the dead victim disappears from the scene, police doubt a crime has been committed. Tory is threatened when she keeps insisting she saw a man killed and the only one who believes her is her neighbor, Jordan Steele. Together, can they solve the mystery of the disappearing body and stay alive?

DEADLY COUNTDOWN, Book Four

Allie Martin, a widow, has a secret protector who manipulates her life without anyone knowing until…

When Remy Broussard, an injured police officer, returns to Port David, Louisiana to visit before his medical leave is over, he discovers his childhood friend, Allie Martin, is being stalked. As Remy protects Allie and tries to find her stalker, they realize their feelings go beyond friendship.

When the stalker is found, they begin to explore the deeper feelings they have for each other, only to have a more sinister threat come between them. Will Allie be able to save Remy before he dies at the hand of a maniac?

DEADLY NOEL, Book Five

Assistant DA, Kira Davis, convicted the wrong man—Gabriel Michaels, a single dad with a young daughter. When new evidence was brought forth, his conviction was overturned, and Gabriel returned home to his ranch to put his life back together. Although Gabriel is free, the murderer of his wife is still out there and resumes killing women. In a desperate alliance, Kira and Gabriel join forces to find the true identity of the person terrorizing their town. Will they be able to forgive the past and find the killer before it's too late?

DEADLY DOSE, Book Six

Drugs. Murder. Redemption.

When Jessie Michaels discovers a letter written to her by her deceased best friend, she is determined to find who murdered Mary Lou, at first thought to be a victim of a serial killer by the police. Jessie's questions lead to an attempt on her life. The last man she wanted to come to her aid was Josh Morgan, who had been instrumental in her brother going to prison. Together they uncover a drug ring that puts them both in danger. Will Jessie and Josh find the killer? Love? Or will one of them fall victim to a DEADLY DOSE?

DEADLY LEGACY, Book Seven

Legacy of Secrets. Threats and Danger. Second Chances.

Down on her luck, single mom, Lacey St. John, believes her life has finally changed for the better when she receives an inheritance from a wealthy stranger. Her ancestral home she'd thought forever lost has been transformed into a lucrative bed and breakfast guaranteed to bring much-needed financial security. Her happiness is complete until strange happenings erode her sense of well being. When her life is threatened, she turns to neighbor, Sheriff Ryan McNeil, for help. He promises to solve the mystery of who's ruining her newfound peace of mind, but when her troubles escalate to the point that her every move leads to danger, she's unsure who to trust. Is the strong, capable neighbor she's falling for as amazing as he seems? Or could he be the man who wants her dead?

DEADLY NIGHT, SILENT NIGHT, Book Eight

Revenge. Sabotage. Second Chances.

Widow Rebecca Howard runs a successful store chain that is being targeted during the holiday season. Detective Alex Kincaid, best friends with Rebecca's twin brother, is investigating the hacking of the store's computer system. When the attacks become personal, Alex must find the assailant before Rebecca, the woman he's falling in love with, is murdered.

DEADLY FIRES, Book Nine

Second Chances. Revenge. Arson.

A saboteur targets Alexia Richards and her family company. As the incidents become more lethal, Alexia must depend on a former Delta Force soldier, Cole Knight, a man from her past that she loved. When their son died in a fire, their grief and anger drove them apart. Can Alexia and Cole work through their pain and join forces to find the person who wants her dead?

DEADLY SECRETS, Book Ten

Secrets. Murder. Reunion.

Sarah St. John, an FBI profiler, finally returns home after fifteen years for her niece's wedding. But in less than a day, Sarah's world is shattered when her niece is kidnapped the night before her vows. Sarah can't shake the feeling her own highly personal reason for leaving Hunter Davis at the altar is now playing out again in this nightmarish scene with her niece.

Sarah has to work with Detective Hunter Davis, her ex-fiancé, to find her niece before the young woman becomes the latest victim of a serial killer. Sarah must relive part of her past in order to assure there is a future for her niece and herself. Can Sarah and Hunter overcome their painful past and work together before the killer strikes again?

About the Author

Margaret Daley, a *USA Today's* Bestselling author of over 105 books (five million plus sold worldwide), has been married for over forty-seven years and is a firm believer in romance and love. When she isn't traveling or being with her two granddaughters, she's writing love stories, often with a suspense/mystery thread and corralling her cats that think they rule her household. To find out more about Margaret visit her website at www.margaretdaley.com.

Facebook:
www.facebook.com/margaretdaleybooks

Twitter:
twitter.com/margaretdaley

Goodreads:
www.goodreads.com/author/Margaret_Daley

Link to sign up for my newsletter on front page of website: www.margaretdaley.com

Made in the USA
Middletown, DE
17 August 2019